LADY GODIVA;

OR,

PEEPING TOM OF COVENTRY.

ILLUSTRATED.

LONDON: 145, FLEET-STREET, E.C.

1869.

LADY GODIVA;

OR, PEEPING TOM OF COVENTRY.

LADY GODIVA ON HER WAY THROUGH COVENTRY

CHAPTER I.

THE MISCHIEVOUS BOYS IN THE MARKET-PLACE —DESCRIPTION OF PEEPING TOM, WHO FINDS A PIN STUCK IN THE WRONG PLACE—TOM HAS A FIGHT WITH SLEEPY JOE, AND RECEIVES A "SMELLER."

THE ancient city of Coventry was in a state of dire commotion; men and women, boys and girls—in fact, the entire population, seemed possessed of the spirit of disorder.

As usual, the great place of public resort was the market-place, and there assembled round the most attractive spot, the market inn, were congregated, in addition to the miscellaneous crowd, the oracles and gossips of the town.

Of these the principal were stalwart Ironbrace the blacksmith, Spout the tinker, Chipper the mason, Oxgall the butcher, Bungs the landlord, and last, not least, Tom Winker, or, as he was nick-named, Peeping Tom of Coventry.

No. 1.

This last individual was supposed to be slightly deficient in that particular part where the brains are usually supposed to be found; he was a curious compound of simplicity and cunning, cowardice and rashness, yet not quite wise enough to be a fool, and too constantly falling into scrapes to be called a coward.

He was a kind of plaything to the entire town, who encouraged him in his peculiarities for the pleasure of laughing at him; and he was an invaluable treasure to the Coventry boys, who were then, as they are now, fond of mischief, and who seized upon Tom in their expeditions and made him the catspaw, as the monkey did the cat in the fable, to pick the chestnuts out of the fire for them to devour.

Tom Winker seemed to thrive upon his adventures.

He was short and dumpy, with a good-natured, stupid face, like a pancake, that smiled all over at the smallest opportunity; he was supposed to have had a father and mother at some time or other, but, as no living relative claimed him but an ancient female whom he called "Granny," his ancestral descent, like his age, was a matter of entire speculation.

Amongst the crowd, then, there was Tom, as usual, surrounded by his friends the boys—those mischievous boys who, even in those times, before trousers were invented, or "bluchers" and "lace-ups" were thought of, or "wide-awakes" decorated juvenile "nobs" (although they were quite wide awake enough), had the audacity, in very defiance of all established rules, to make faces round the corner at the tax-collector, and *chaff* the crier, to say nothing of the trumpeter, whom they imitated, much to their own gratification and the intense disgust of that strong-winded (not minded) personage.

There was, then, what might be termed a general "row" on a small scale in the market-place; everybody grumbled, everybody spoke at once, but yet, amidst the din and *furore*, special ejaculations were distinctly heard.

"I shan't pay the infernal tax!" growled stalwart Ironbrace, the blacksmith.

"I'll die fust!" chimed in Chipper.

"I'd sooner be knocked on the head!" said Oxgall.

Poppyhead, the apothecary, vowed he'd sooner be pounded to death in a mortar, if one could be found big enough; and Bungs, the landlord, declared that a *watery* grave in one of his own ale barrels would be infinitely preferable.

Not supposing that this last speaker intended to be sarcastic upon the liquor he sold, we may presume he meant *beery* grave—at all events, he said watery.

"Ee-ee!" cried Tom, bolting a mouthful of gingerbread and coming in last; "I ain't a-goin' to pay no tax; I sat down on a paper o' tin tacks yesterday an' tore my breeches. I'd sooner have old mother Doublechin's skewer poked in my eye again, for peeping through her keyhole while she was a boilin' up her conjurations in the large iron pot."

"Ha! ha! ha!" laughed the crowd.

"Ee! ee! ee!" roared Tom, who always laughed when anybody else laughed, and always the loudest. His mirth was suddenly stopped by a yell—"Oh! o-h!"

Dare Devil Dick, one of his juvenile patrons,

had slipped behind and quietly stuck a good old English "corking pin" up to the head in a certain available part of Tom's anatomy.

"What's the matter?" said Quicksilver Harry another of his companions.

"Oh! oh! oh!" cried Tom; "something pricks me dreadful behind;" and clapping his hand to the offended part, he, after some investigation, produced the instrument of torture.

"There, now!" he exclaimed, holding it between his finger and thumb, "if that ain't too bad, I don't know what is."

"Oh, what a shame!" cried the treacherous Dick; "that *is too* bad!"

"And to stick it into him behind, too!' chimed in Harry. "That was you, Mister Sleepy Joe," he continued, pointing to a drowsy youth, who was at that moment endeavouring to masticate a mouthful of a certain compound, which, in these modern times, would be recognised as "black-jack" or "stick-jaw."

"Oh, what a crammer!" returned Joe, indignantly. "Why, I wasn't near him—was I, Bill?" appealing to a thin lad who had been cracking nuts, and had neither seen nor heard anything of the occurrence.

Bill was about to state this fact, when a nudge from Dick gave him his *cue*, and the deceitful urchin settled Joe completely by saying—

"Why, of course you were; you asked that woman there for a pin, and I saw you stick it into Tom behind."

"Oh! oh! oh!" resounded from the boys on all sides.

Poor Joe was overwhelmed by numbers and stick-jaw, and grinned and gasped helplessly.

"Look at him," cried the boys; "look how red he's got in the face. Don't stand it, Tom. I wouldn't if I was you."

The young rascals were bursting to get up a fight.

"You don't mean to say you *are* going to stand it, do you?" inquired Dick, giving Tom a sharp slap on the wounded part, just to stir him up a bit.

"Oh, don't, please," cried Tom, shrinking; "don't slap me there; that's where the pin went."

"You're not going to stand it, I say?" repeated the pugilistic Dick.

"Well, I don't know," replied Tom, simply; "I think I must stand it, I can't sit down," he added, passing his hand soothingly over that region which would have been particularly affected by the operation of sitting.

"I'd knock his head off his shoulders if I were you," urged Harry.

"Would you, though?" said Tom. "I don't know whether I could knock it off," he continued, dubiously; "heads are stuck on so precious tight. Not all heads — broom-heads ain't. The last time I tried to whack our cat with granny's broom, the top flew off and went slap through"—

"Never mind granny's broom," interrupted the bloodthirsty Dick, who would not diverge from his point; "you've been insulted by that Joe there, and if yer don't do something we shall all think you're afraid of him—shan't we, boys?"

"Ay, ay, ay," resounded on all sides.

"I ain't afraid of him," said Tom, surreptitiously conveying a handful of gingerbread into his mouth ; "I ain't afraid of nothink."

"At all events, if he is, I'm not," exclaimed Joe, who, though rather slow, was no coward, and who, having released his teeth from the sticky mass by which they had been fettered, was now able to express himself.

"If you say," he commenced, addressing the slanderous Bill, "that I stuck that pin into Tom, I say you're not speaking the truth."

"Now, then, go on," cried Dick and Harry in a whisper to Tom, pushing him forward ; "say he is."

"I say he is," answered Tom, obediently.

"Oh, I understand," returned Sleepy Joe, with a smile and a curl of his lip ; "you're edging on poor stupid Tom to fight me ; well, then, I shan't fight *him*, I shall fight Bill for telling lies about me."

"Very well," said Bill, coolly cracking his last nut. "I'm ready."

"No, he ain't," interposed Tom, who at last took it for granted that there was a stern necessity for his fighting somebody ; "he ain't a goin' to fight you ; I'm a goin' to fight you ; I ain't a goin' to let any one fight my battles."

"Bravo ! bravo, Tom !" echoed on all sides.

"Come on," cried Tom, compressing his lips till his mouth appeared to extend from ear to ear, and elevating his eyebrows ; "come on."

Joe, in a very cool and business-like manner, seeing that Tom was determined to proceed to extremities, threw off his jerkin, and *did* come on, assuming an easy attitude, and thinking that a slight visitation, in the shape of a tap on the nose, or a punch in the wind, would, after all, perhaps, be the shortest way of settling matters.

Tom's attitude was sublime.

His fat little legs, or rather his fat little toes, were slightly turned in ; his hair had, for the occasion, whether from the intensity of his chivalrous sensations, or from a cause diametrically opposite, assumed the perpendicular, and each particular root appeared to stand on end like "knots upon the fretful porcupine," and to unite by common consent in a point several inches above his head, giving him an appearance of intensity that was highly comic.

His arms were rounded in front of his body, and his fists, as he felt impressed with the necessity of being as terrible in his motions as possible, went regularly round and round, as though someone had been winding him up behind.

The mischievous boys were in convulsions, but they restrained their mirth, in order that the proceedings might not be interrupted.

"Bravo, Tom !" they cried. "There's an attitude ! Turn your toes in a little more, Tom ; that's it. Bravo !"

Even Joe, as he glanced at his opponent, could not forbear a smile.

"Mind," said he, turning to Bill, " after I've polished off Tom, here, I shall tackle *you*."

"All right, sleepy head," answered Bill.

The polishing prospect seemed to have a quickening effect upon Tom's fists, that were now spinning round with the velocity of a windmill.

"Now then," cried Dare Devil Dick, who was tired of the preliminaries, and wanted to come to business, "time—go on !"

"Come on !" exclaimed Tom, nervously com-pressing his lips, and drawing in his breath through his teeth, producing a sound like that of water gurgling down a sink. "Come on !"

Tom shut his eyes, lowered his head, and made a sudden butt at Joe, in which attempt he was assisted by a lift behind from Dick's foot.

Cool Joe kindly stepped aside, and gave Tom the full benefit of a wooden post, where he had been standing, and against which his head resounded like a skittle-ball.

"Take care, Tom," said one of the facetious youths, who was looking on; "you'll have the clerk of the market after you if you damage the posts in that way."

The blow would have killed any ordinary youth of seventeen (Tom's age was not accurately known ; some said he was seventeen, some thirty, some fifty ; I, therefore, give him the benefit of the doubt, and call him by the former of these ages) ; but Tom had a thick head, and looked upon the episode of the post as a capital joke.

"Ee ! ce ! ee !" he grinned, going up to the post, which was shaky, and moving it from side to side; " that was a one-er, wasn't it ?"

"Time !" cried Dick.

"Look out now !" exclaimed Tom ; and shutting his eyes (he always shut his eyes under such circumstances), and throwing his arms in all directions, he rushed once more upon his antagonist, who quietly extended his arm with his clenched fist at the end of it for the especial accommodation of Tom's nose, which came into immediate collision, and received what is usually termed a decided *smeller*.

Tom, who was only invulnerable on his nob, was done.

"Oh ! oh ! oh ! my nose !" he blubbered vociferously, performing a kind of fat Indian war-dance in the extremity of his anguish; "he's knocked my nose down my throat, I think ;" and, as if to be quite sure that such was not the case, he swallowed a large lump of gingerbread.

The boys gathered round Tom, and administered consolation in the shape of nuts and sweetstuff, whilst Joe, in an unruffled, dogged tone said to Bill—

"Now, Mister Bill, it's your turn."

Bill's preparations were soon made, and fight number two was about to commence, when the sound of a trumpet was heard at the extreme end of the market, and then the voice of the crier, " O yes ! O yes ! O yes !"

This put an immediate stop to the proceedings, and the eyes and attention of everybody, which had been for a long time diverted by the freaks of the boys, were now turned in the direction whence the sounds proceeded.

CHAPTER II.

THE TAX-COLLECTOR APPLIES FOR THE TAX, AND IS REFUSED—ARRIVAL OF THE NORMAN CAPTAIN AND HIS TROOP—THE SPARK TO THE TRAIN—RIOT, AND DEFEAT OF THE TROOPERS —THE RESOLVE OF THE REBELS.

THE personages who almost immediately after entered the market-place were recognised as Grippin, the tax-collector of the worshipful Leofric, Earl of Mercia and Lord of Coventry, attended by the trumpeter and crier.

The very sight of these individuals appeared offensive, and the murmurings and grumblings that arose as they approached proved how obnoxious the tax in question must have been.

Grippin and his satellites advanced to the centre of the market-place, and there halted.

Oh ! what a chance for the boys, who, crouching down behind out of sight, made their remarks indiscriminately.

" Bravo, Fat-head !" cried one.

This was a direct personal allusion to the tax-collector, who had a thick, bullet head.

" *Grippin, Grippin, stole the poor woman's drippin',*" declaimed another in doggrel rhyme.

The tax-collector, whose ear had caught a portion of the above, looked round angrily, but in vain, to detect the impertinent speaker.

The trumpeter sounded his trumpet.

" Go it, buster !" cried Dare Devil Dick.

" O yes ! O yes ! O yes !" uttered the monotonous crier.

" O no ! O no ! O no !" echoed Peeping Tom, who had forgotten his damaged nose, and was enjoying the fun immensely.

" Order !" shouted the tax-collector.

" Ordure !" bawled Tom.

The townsmen, however, were anxious to hear what Grippin had to say, and Oxgall the butcher, dropping upon Tom as he delivered the last exclamation, gave him a quiet wring of the ear till he thought it was coming out by the root, and administering a kick in the corking pin department, sent him howling to his friends, and the proceedings were allowed to go on.

The crowd gathered round.

" Citizens of Coventry," commenced Grippin, " and vassals of the most *puissant* and noble Leofric, Earl of Mercia, seeing that our gracious sovereign, Richard of the Lion Heart, is about to lead his armies to the Holy Land to do battle with the Infidels, and it seeming fit to the noble earl your master to enlist under his royal banner, he doth therefore command the immediate payment of the tax which hath been previously proclaimed, namely : one mark for every man, ten shillings for every woman, and five shillings for every child throughout the city, as a means whereby he may equip a force that shall do honour to his own dignity, and reflect credit upon you his liege vassals. Answer, shall he have it ?"

" O yes ! O yes ! O yes !" bawled the crier, who woke up suddenly from a nap, and dropped in his interjections in the wrong place.

" No ! no ! no !" was the furious and contradictory response from a hundred throats.

Grippin, having first impaled the crier with a piercing glance, turned his angry face to the mob.

" Are ye rebellious ?" he cried.

" Yes, we are !" shouted a score of voices.

" Have ye no care for the honour and credit of your city ?" inquired the indignant tax-collector.

" We care about the honour of our city," cried Ironbrace the blacksmith, " but not about the crusades ; what are the Infidels to us ?"

" Ay, ay ! what ?" echoed his companions.

" Do they not assault the Pilgrims ?"

" What have we to do with them ?"

" They are Christians, and must not be insulted !"

" We are Christians, and must not be starved !"

" You are English, and must pay the tax !" cried the irritated collector.

" O yes ! O yes ! O yes !" called the crier.

" Silence !" shouted Grippin, turning furiously upon this luckless official, who, from the confused din, and the nervousness attendant upon the prospects of a brawl, had become somewhat wandering in his mental faculties ; " it is your confounded ' O yes ! O yes !' that has put the people in a bad humour."

" O ye "— he was about to reply, as a matter of course, but pulled himself up suddenly and swallowed his words in a slight cough.

" It's not he that puts us out of humour," explained Oxgall. " Here, lad, drink," he continued, passing a tankard of ale to the crier, who, nothing loath, plunged into it head foremost, and was seen no more for some seconds. " It's you and your infernal tax that upsets us, and nothing else," wound up the butcher.

" Not my tax, fellow !" answered the incensed Grippin, " but his lordship, the Earl of Mercia's tax."

" It's a cursed grasping tax, and we refuse to pay it !" cried a score of voices.

" Hooray ! hooray !" cried another voice, and looking up, the crowd beheld Mr. Thomas Winker, mounted on one of the door porticos, waving his hand energetically. " That's right, fellow-citizens and brother smuts," he cried. " Don't pay ; I won't ! Here," he suddenly ejaculated, as though a new idea had flashed across his addled brain, " I'll settle it for you. I'll go an' tell the earl you're hard up, and can't pay," and with these words, he scrambled down from the portico, and ran off as fast as his legs could carry him.

" Let the idiot go !" cried Ironbrace, annoyed at the interruption ; " and do you," addressing his words to Grippin, " go and tell the earl, if he wants this money, he'd better come and take it. And now begone, or you may find it the worse for you."

" O ye "——

The crier was about to burst out, but he recollected that he was not to speak, and retired within himself immediately.

A Babel of confusion increased on every side. Various suggestions as to the propriety of hanging the collector, blowing up the trumpeter, and smothering the crier, were distinctly heard, and it seemed probable that the agent would have retired with marks of a different description from those he sought, when an armed troop appeared at the end of the market-place, and approached the spot where the announcement had just been made.

This was no other than the earl's Norman captain, Routier, who had been despatched in consequence of the resistance of the people to the demanded tax, to enforce it in a more summary manner than by a mere verbal application.

At this period the Saxons, as a conquered race, hated the Normans as their conquerors ; and the Normans, in their turn, despised the Saxons as their slaves.

Consequently, the approaching cavalcade, with a Norman at their head, was the most inopportune arrival that could possibly have occurred, inasmuch as it increased the irritation of minds already inflamed.

The murmurs of subdued wrath gradually increased in volume from the time when the troopers, twenty in number, first appeared, until the moment when they drew up in the centre of the market-place.

Captain Routier glanced down upon the crowd, and beholding nothing but looks expressive of discontent and hatred, he exclaimed fiercely—

"What is the meaning of these sour faces and knitted brows?"

"*He* knows," said Ironbrace, in a tone equally fierce, indicating the tax-collector, by an abrupt nod. "You'd better ask him; our breath's too valuable to be thrown away in answering idle questions."

Captain Routier, fixing a momentary glance of indignant contempt upon Ironbrace for his disrespectful reply, bent down in his saddle, and spoke in a low tone to Grippin, who, having delivered his information, departed, accompanied by the trumpeter and crier.

The information the captain received did not appear to increase the placidity of his temper, for he raised himself in a few moments, with a flushed visage and a frowning brow.

"I understand," he said, in a stern voice, "you refuse to pay this tax?"

"We do!" resounded on every side.

The Norman's lip curled contemptuously.

"To your refusal," he continued, "churls, as ye are, I have but one reply—you *must* pay it!"

"And to your *must*," slowly replied Ironbrace, "*we* have only one reply,—we *won't* pay it!"

"I am empowered to enforce compliance," said the Norman, with irritating pertinacity.

"Enforce it, then!" shouted several, "and see what will come of it!"

"Down with the Norman tyrants!" cried others. "This is their work!"

"Ay, ay," chimed in a volley of fresh voices; "they're a set of lazy vermin. They won't work themselves, and they'd have us industrious English keep them while they play. Down with them! down with the accursed breed!" rang through the air on all sides.

Several stones were hurled at the troopers, but without doing any serious injury.

Routier, the captain, seeing that matters were taking a serious turn, cried out—

"Disperse! To your homes! Reflect on what has been said, and to-morrow"——

His words were drowned by groans, execrations, and jeers.

"Our answer to-morrow will be the same as it is to-day. No!" they shouted

"Do you hear me?" cried the captain.

A groan of contempt was the only reply.

Routier turned pale with rage.

"If you move not ere the clock yonder strikes eleven (it then wanted five minutes of the hour), I will hasten your departure with the points of my troopers' swords," growled Routier, pointing to the clock.

A laugh of scorn was thrown at him in answer.

The five minutes passed, the clock struck; but far from dispersing, the crowd thronged around the mounted troop more densely than ever.

The Norman bit his nether lip with wrath.

"These English swine!" he muttered between his teeth. "There is no bending—we must crush them. Ho, Guiscard!" he shouted, "fall in! clear the market."

At the word of command the troopers, forming a square, urged on their horses with the inten-

tion of forcing back those of the multitude who would be forced, and riding down those who would not.

But this was a crisis when the English mettle was to be tested, and the troopers might as well have tried to ride down a stone wall.

The screams of women and children now mingled with the execrations of the men, who pressed forward resolutely upon the troopers.

The captain could no longer control his fury. "Back, dogs!" he cried; and as he spoke he struck the foremost of the insurgents a blow in the face with his sword.

That blow was electric; it was the spark that exploded the train of popular fury. A wild yell rose in the air; the dense mass, like a raging sea, poured in on all sides. The horses, unable to stir, became unmanageable, and reared, falling back upon their fellows; stones darkened the air; whilst the troopers, bleeding and powerless, essayed in vain to pierce the ranks.

Their captain tried to enforce a hearing. He might as well have sought to drown the thunder as it rolled through the vault above; his voice was drowned in the cry—"Down with the enslavers! Down with the Norman myrmidons!" And with these adjurations the assault began.

Notwithstanding the weapons they carried, the soldiers were comparatively powerless.

So closely were they packed that they embarrassed each other; the prancings and plungings of their horses adding to their confusion. In a few moments there was not one of the troop that was not unhorsed, from the captain downwards.

What they suffered at the hands of the exasperated mob may be gathered from the fact that, at ten minutes past eleven, ten men lay crushed and brained upon the ground of the market-place; whilst the rest were so severely injured that they were at the mercy of the mob.

The Norman captain, maimed and bleeding, demanded a parley.

The immediate vengeance of the multitude being satiated, it was granted.

"Your numbers have overpowered us," he said faintly. "Suffer us to retire."

"Ay! ay! retire," answered Oxgall, the butcher, who had felled three troopers with his own hand as though they had been so many oxen; "and tell the worshipful earl what has happened. It'll help to teach him what he may expect if he thinks to ride over us rough-shod."

The wounded troopers got away as they best could amidst the groans and jeers of the mob, carrying with them the mangled bodies of their comrades.

No sooner had they departed than Ironbrace, who appeared to be the leading man of the people, probably because he was the strongest, which, in those days of might over right, was a great virtue, stepped forward.

"Now's the time, fellow-citizens, to strike," he cried. "We've given these troopers a lesson of what we can do when our blood's up, and we must take care the lesson is not forgotten."

"Ay! ay!" shouted a hundred voices.

"Let us come at once to the castle," he continued; "and if his earlship talks about enforcing this tax, we'll have the walls down about his ears."

A shout of unanimous acquiescence followed this brief harangue.

"Arm yourselves with whatever weapons come first to hand, and I'll lead you on; we'll teach this earl to think twice before he asks once in future."

Another vociferous cheer rent the air, and with loud cries, "To the castle! to the castle!" the mob scattered in every direction to provide themselves with such means of defence as they were able to muster.

Ironbrace, their leader, hastened to his shop, and arming himself with a formidable-looking knife, which he thrust into a leathern sheath at his side, he shouldered his hammer, and locking up his shop, departed to the scene of action.

CHAPTER III.

PEEPING TOM CLIMBS OVER THE CASTLE WALL —THE FRUITS OF STEALING FRUIT—HE GETS OUT OF THE CASTLE AND LETS IN THE REBELS—LADY GODIVA'S PROMISE.

LEOFRIC, from the usually patient submission of the people to his sometimes rapacious demands, expected an easy acquiescence in the present instance, especially when those demands were backed by a body of twenty armed and mounted men.

He accordingly relaxed a little in the wrath which the announcement of their refusal to pay the tax had occasioned, and sat down to breakfast, which consisted of a boar's head, moistened with copious draughts of ale and Rhenish wine.

His repast was scarcely finished when a violent amalgamation of sounds, composed of the barking of hounds, the angry voices of men, and the cries of one whom they had captured, fell upon the earl's ear.

"What, in the name of all the saints, is the matter?" exclaimed the earl to Hubert, his seneschal, who was in attendance.

"I will see, my lord," answered the old man, and immediately left the room.

My readers will not be surprised to hear that this uproar was occasioned by our friend Peeping Tom, who was mad enough for any absurdity, and who acting up to the promise he made on the portico, had set off at full speed to the castle, to state the general resolution of the people to the earl.

Having arrived there, he wandered about until he reached a spot that did not appear to be very vigilantly watched, and then climbing a tree that grew close by, he swung his fat body over the wall, and alighted in the midst of a bed of stinging-nettles.

"Tin-tacks! corking-pins and stinging-nettles!" he cried, springing up and repeating the war-dance, with the addition of an imaginary solo on the "bones" with his hands, which he shook frantically, whilst his eyes were almost starting out of his head.

"Oh! oh! oh!" he cried, "don't they bite!"

After a few moments the pain somewhat abated, and he was able to look round at the he had fallen.

It was a garden at the rear of the castle, a spot evidently devoted to fruit and vegetables.

Tom's greedy eyes fell upon some gooseberry bushes, and all his philanthropic resolutions were dispelled at once.

Taxes and all such absurd nonsense vanished from his thoughts, and he became absorbed in the realities of the tempting fruit just under his nose.

Tom had his weaknesses, and gooseberries was one. Without more ado he commenced, utterly regardless of everything but eating as much as he possibly could.

After some time he paused; he was tired of picking; to be tired of eating was a state of feeling which he had never yet experienced.

"Phew!" said he, wiping his forehead, which was moist with his exertions. "I wonder how many quarts I've swallowed; I'm tired of gooseberries. I wonder whether they've got any peaches?"

He examined the walls.

"Yes, decidedly, there were peaches."

In an incredibly short space of time he had devoured several dozen, when Delve, the gardener, who happened to be at work at some distance, cast his eyes in that direction, and caught sight of Tom, who was remorselessly tearing the luscious peaches from their stalks as though they had been blackberries.

Delve was aghast with rage and horror.

"Hollo!" he roared, at the top of his voice; "d'ye hear, you thieving scoundrel? Heigh!"

Tom, startled in the midst of his feast by this stentorian voice, bolted a peach, stone and all, that nearly choked him, and in his haste to depart, plunged head first into a cucumber frame.

The gardener, half-frantic, rushed to a stable close by for the dog.

"Here, Nero! Nero!" he shouted; "here's a wild thief dewourin' the peaches and smashin' the cowcumbers. Dig your teeth into him!"

The rattling of a chain and the excited barking of a dog were heard, which sounds increased the agitation of Tom Winker.

"Oh! my goodness gracious!" he cried, scrambling to his feet in a state of abject terror, "wherever shall I go? Cuss the gooseberries! Cuss the peaches!"

The barking of the dog and the raving of the incensed gardener increased.

Tom found himself in front of a grape-vine.

Here was a chance to climb it and have the laugh both of man and beast.

He commenced; the task was easy. One—two—three—four steps up, and he was out of the reach of the fangs of the fierce bloodhound that came tearing up to the spot, his hungry jaws wide apart, and his formidable fangs apparently thirsting to lay hold of Tom anywhere.

"Come off the vine!" roared the gardener, in a perfect agony at seeing his pet tree ruthlessly crushed and scraped by Tom's hands and feet. "Come down, you sanguinary willin! Come down!"

Tom, however, was near the top, and in spite of his past fears could not resist the impulse to turn round and grin at the irate agriculturist beneath.

"Come down, scoundrel!" cried the latter, shaking his fist at him furiously.

"Don't you wish you may get it?" replied impudent Tom.

The bloodhound, chafed to madness at seeing his prey so near without being able to get the smallest nibble at him, growled, whined, and barked incessantly, springing up every now and then at Tom's heels, but without effect.

"Ugh! you savage, ugly brute!" said Tom, giving him a kick on the jaw, as he made another spring, which sent him howling backwards.

"Try again, Nero! At him again—good dog!" raved the man, encouraging the fierce animal.

"Boo!" cried Tom, making faces at the gardener; "boo! you old watering-pot!"

This was too much for human endurance. The gardener rushed towards a rake, and advanced to inflict summary vengeance.

"Oho! it's rakes now, is it?" ejaculated Tom. "Let him come, I'm ready for him."

He calculated the time and distance to a nicety, and as the furious agriculturist approached, he grasped the vine, and made a spring to the top of the wall.

At least, such was his intention; it, however, happened, so fate willed it, that some of the nails that supported the vine gave way, and the branches to which he clung, loosing from the wall, he had no time or power to make a fresh hold, and after hanging for a second, as it were, suspended in the balance, the centre of gravity triumphed, and Peeping Tom fell with a crash to the ground, dragging the grape-vine with him, in a shower of dust, earwigs, and spiders, which came down with him.

Then came the succession of shrieks, growlings, and execrations, that had startled the earl, and had it not been for the sudden arrival of Hubert with two troopers, it is more than probable Nero would there and then have bolted Tom, even though he had died of indigestion afterwards.

As it was, the seneschal ordered the dog to be called off, and being apprised of the facts, conducted the trespasser to the earl's presence.

The earl, having been informed of the assaults committed upon his gooseberries, peaches, and grape-vine, was naturally indignant.

"Knave!" he exclaimed, "you shall be taught there is a penalty attached to these paltry thefts."

"I didn't come after the gooseberries," blubbered Tom, "nor the peaches, nor the grape-vines either; I didn't, upon my honour!"

"Your lordship," said the gardener, "the fellow lies. I saw him eating them with my own eyes."

"Oh!" affirmed Tom, in a tone of injured innocence, accompanied by a fresh torrent of tears; "oh, what a wicked story! I haven't ate one, your noble lordship."

"He means," said Delve, "he hasn't left one. He has almost cleared the tree, and torn the grape-vine from the wall."

"Oh! has he?" exclaimed the earl; "then we will nail him up instead."

Tom was getting desperate, and suddenly bethought him of the original purpose that brought him to the castle.

"Your lordship," he cried, "don't nail me up! I came here on very important business—I did, indeed!"

"What business!" inquired the earl, sternly.

Having already told several lies, Tom thought one or two more would not make much difference.

"Speak!" said the earl.

"I came to pay the tax," replied Tom, boldly.

"Pay it, then," exclaimed Leofric.

Tom felt in all his pockets; but the idea of finding any coin there was utterly fabulous.

"Make haste," urged the earl.

"I—I can't find it!" cried Tom, bursting into a fresh agony of grief; "I must ha' dropped it while I was hangin' on to the grape-vine; or p'raps that ferocious dog went and swallowed it!"

"Bah!" exclaimed the earl, impatiently. "Take the fellow away; and, as it appears he has eaten sufficient fruit to kill half a dozen varlets of his condition, let him have a pint of rhubarb, and be thankful we are so mindful of his health."

But Tom, who abhorred everything in the shape of physic, was by no means disposed to take his pint without a struggle, and made one last effort.

"Your lordship won't miss my poor little coin," he said, in a whining tone, "when your collector brings you the collections of the whole city."

"What, have they agreed to pay?" cried the earl, eagerly.

"I believe you, they has too," replied Tom; "when I come away the money was a pourin' in like anythin', so I thought I'd come an' tell your lordship."

This was hitting the right nail on the head. The earl was delighted.

"This is news, indeed!" he cried. "I forgive you, fellow, in the matter of the peaches and the vine, and hold you free yourself from the tax for your intelligence."

"Thankee, yer lordship," said Tom, humbly, "an' now, if you please, may I go home? Granny will be waitin' for me."

"Yes, go my good fellow," replied Leofric, giving him a gold coin from his pouch; "and thanks for your information."

It was rather unfortunate for Tom, though a just punishment for his falsehoods, that, as he was going out, Grippin rushed in, in a state of great excitement.

Tom, who knew his fate if he remained, put the coin in his pocket, and made a desperate bolt between the collector's legs, overturning him instantly.

As soon as the bewildered agent was set upon his legs, the earl demanded—

"Where is the money?"

"What money, your lordship?" he inquired.

"The collection—the tax!" answered the earl, hastily.

"I have none, my lord. The people are insolent, and refuse to pay; I apprehend a riot."

"Then," shouted the earl, furiously, "that varlet lied; follow him. I'll hang the dog from my castle turret."

This command was about to be put into execution when a terrific yell, that shook the castle to its foundation, caused a general pause. Hardly had they recovered from their momentary surprise, when the alarm-bell sounded, and Routier, the Norman captain, pale and bleeding, staggered into the apartment.

"Save yourself, my lord," he cried, faintly. "The people are up in arms. Ten of our men have fallen beneath their hands, and the rebels are even now at the castle gates."

Having thus spoken, he sank down exhausted.

"Ha!" cried the stout earl, starting up' his cheeks flushing and his eyes darting fire "do these dogs think to frighten me by barking in my ears? By heaven! they shall find that I am made of different mettle. Ho, there!" he shouted, as he seized a ponderous mace bristling with spikes; "call out the archers; bid them line the walls; we'll send these curs howling to their kennels or their graves ere sunset."

Throwing his mace over his shoulder, he was about to hasten on to the battlements, when once more a shout, more wild and terrible than the former, thundered through the air; a sound like a rushing torrent followed, that speedily developed itself in the form of the hurried tramp of approaching footsteps.

"Hark!" cried the earl; "by hell! they have forced the gates!" and as he spoke a dense mass of insurgents, whom our friend Peeping Tom in letting himself out had admitted, poured in a resistless stream into the very chamber where he stood.

The angry noble, like a lion at bay, faced the heated, angry mob, with a resolution equal to their own.

"Keep back!" he cried to the foremost ranks, brandishing the formidable weapon he grasped; "keep back! or by all the saints, I warn ye the first that comes within my reach shall require masses for his soul ere he be a moment older."

The appearance of the earl, who was above six feet in height, with limbs like a Hercules, brought the rebels to a temporary pause.

"Why are you here, and thus armed?" he inquired, in a voice hoarse with passion.

"To ask if you withdraw this tax?" answered Ironbrace the blacksmith, who with begrimed hands and face, and brow streaked with sweat, that gave him the appearance of a formidable Vulcan, leant for an instant on his ponderous hammer.

"No! thou base-born hind!" foamed the incensed earl, who was utterly insensible at that moment even to his own personal safety; "rather will I double—treble it! Retire, you pack of slaves!" he shouted.

"Advance!" cried the blacksmith.

"Down with the tyrant!" echoed on all sides.

The smith raised his hammer, and rushed forward; but the earl, planting his foot firmly on the ground, received the blow upon his mace, and, by a sudden jerk, threw the instrument, the head of which was caught by the iron spikes, several yards over his head; then, brandishing the formidable weapon he carried as though it had been a reed, he was about to rush headlong into the midst of the throng, when the Lady Godiva, her beautiful hair falling in dishevelled confusion over her shoulders, and her eyes wild with terror, suddenly appeared from a small arched door on one side of the chamber, and threw herself upon her knees between her husband and his rebellious vassals.

"Forbear! forbear! for heaven's sake, dear love," she cried, in a voice trembling with excitement; "this contest is cruel and unnatural; it is the children fighting against the parent, the parent against the children!"

"The noble lady says truly," murmured some voices. "It is so."

"Retire peaceably, I beseech you," she continued, with intense earnestness, "and I will entreat your lord in your behalf."

"Let his lordship forego the tax," cried a score of voices, "and we will depart."

"I will ask him now here in the presence of you all," said the Lady Godiva.

The insurgents looked on in silence as the countess approached the earl, who stood with knitted brows moodily in the centre of the apartment, and knelt before him.

"My liege lord," she exclaimed, humbly, "grant, as a boon to your loving wife, exemption to these, our people, from this grievous burden."

"They are rebels," replied the earl, moodily, turning away from the beautiful supplicant, though, in the desperate crisis to which events had arrived, he was not in his heart sorry to behold her in the attitude of a mediator.

"Hear me, my lord," she cried, entreatingly; "I will not rise till thou hast promised to grant my request."

The earl turned and looked down into the supplicating eyes of his lovely wife. After a pause, he said—

"Are you willing to purchase this boon, Godiva?"

"At any price consistent with my lord's honour and my own," she replied.

"Wouldst thou, then," continued the earl, "if I revoke this tax, ride naked through the town in the sight of these rebels for whom you plead?"

The countess paused, whilst a deep blush overspread her features; it was, however, but for an instant; her intentions were too pure for shame to tinge, and raising her clear eyes of violet blue to her husband's face, she inquired—

"Will you grant me permission so to do?"

"I will," answered Leofric.

"Then I, on my part, promise to do as thou hast said, if heaven spares me till to-morrow," she replied.

"And I, on my part," said the earl, "do pledge my word to keep my promise to thee."

Loud shouts of triumph followed this arrangement.

"Long live the noble Lady Godiva!" "Blessings on her beauty!" rose on the air in all directions; and the mob, having gained the day, turned their faces once more towards home, shouting joyously as they went.

As they approached the gates, to their great surprise, they discovered the unfortunate Tom, who, when he opened the portal to let himself out, little guessed what was in store for him.

No sooner had he drawn the massive bolts, than the entire crowd burst in and overwhelmed him.

In the excitement he was not even seen.

The fact was, he was on the ground, undergoing a summary process of kicking, pressing, and trampling.

It was in vain he roared and yelled; whenever he opened his mouth somebody immediately put his foot in it, and by the time about five hundred pairs of heels had passed over him, Tom became painfully alive to the fact that *something* had disagreed with him.

Terrible pains racked him; remorseless imps inside appeared to be screwing him up to the highest pitch of human endurance.

"It's them gooseberries," he thought. "I

LADY GODIVA;

OR, PEEPING TOM OF COVENTRY.

"DOWN WITH THE TYRANT!"

knows it is—I ate a pretty good lot; or it might be the peaches; I remember bolting one, stone and all."

Here a violent succession of spasmodic twinges seized him.

"Oh! oh! oh!" he groaned, as a dreadful nausea came upon him. "It's wind, I think," he groaned, piteously.

His conscience smote him as he remembered how often he had made a jest of his poor old granny under a similar affliction.

"Cuss the wind!" he cried. "Oh! oh! Poor old granny! Oh! cuss the gooseberries! Oh! cuss the peaches! Oh! what a 'orrid screwy pain! Oh, oh!" he groaned, "will anybody be kind enough to stamp upon me, and put me out of my misery?"

This request was not complied with, and, as he appeared to have had a receipt in full for all his mischief without any more stamps being required, he was set upon his feet and led away by his two dear friends, Dare Devil Dick and

Quicksilver Harry, who did all they could to put him to rights by dropping him accidentally (on purpose) some dozen times on the road home, which shaking answered the purpose of an emetic, and rendered a visit to Poppyhead, the apothecary, unnecessary, Tom, by the time he arrived at the town, being completely restored.

CHAPTER IV.

PEEPING TOM TREATS HIS FRIENDS, AND GETS A DROP TOO MUCH HIMSELF—ARRIVAL OF THREE RUFFIANS—SUDDEN APPEARANCE OF THE YOUNG STRANGER—TOM INSULTS THE DUTCHMAN.

IT may easily be imagined that after the morning's excitement everything like work was suspended for the rest of the day.

Everybody assembled at the market inn, and the bottles and barrels of Bungs, the host, were in constant requisition.

In the course of the afternoon Ironbrace and Chipper, who had been retained at the castle to repair some damage the gates and masonry adjacent had sustained, joined their companions in high spirits.

"By the mass!" said Ironbrace, "the Lady Godiva is a right noble dame!"

"Ay, marry is she!" joined in Chipper, the mason. She came and looked at us as we worked at the gate, and smiled at us out of her blue eyes, till we were fain to stop our work, and look at her."

"Ee! ee!" grinned Tom, who had been taken home to his granny, and compelled to wash his face and comb his hair, and who now, with his fat cheeks shining and red as the setting sun, surrounded by his friends, the boys, eating gingerbread, and drinking ale, was in his glory.

He had got rid of all his unpleasant sensations, and was now as well as if nothing had occurred.

"Ee! ee! ee!" he grinned, "the Lady Godiva didn't come and look at me when I was in the garden, picking the gooseberries and peaches."

"Why should she look at a fool like you?" said Ironbrace ; "we were hard at work mending the ironwork at the gate."

"You'd never have got inside the gate at all, not one of yer, if I hadn't a' let yer in," replied Tom.

"And a pretty mess you made of it when you opened the gates," remarked Chipper; "it's a wonder you wern't crushed to atoms."

"Ee, ee, ee," grinned Tom ; "it were a wonder, that it were."

"The fact is," said Dare Devil Dick, "Tom had blown himself out so tight with gooseberries and peaches, that he wanted pressing into his proper shape again. Look at him now, he's as graceful as ever."

"Yes," replied Tom, "I'm as wasteful as ever," cramming a lump of gingerbread into his mouth, and taking a long draught of ale to wash it down.

"Wouldn't he make a splendid ale-barrel!" cried Quicksilver Harry, giving Tom a friendly tap on the stomach, which made him open his mouth suddenly, and gasp like an expiring codfish.

Everybody laughed at Tom, who required a good deal of gingerbread to restore his equanimity.

"Did the Lady Godiva give you any of the castle ale?" inquired Bungs of the mason, curiously.

"Ay, marry, that did she!" answered Chipper; "it was ale, too! I always thought you sold good stuff, Master Bungs, but I confess Lady Godiva's ale beats yours hollow."

"Does it?" said the landlord, "then be it known to all present, that the ale you drank up at the castle came out of my cellar."

"Did it, though?" replied the blacksmith ; "then all I've got to say, friend Bungs, is, that in the ale you brew for the earl, you put more malt and less water than in ours."

Again there was a laugh, but this time at the expense of the landlord, who denied the impeachment, and protested he served all his customers, whether lords or commoners, precisely alike.

"D'ye think the Lady Godiva drinks ale?"

"Of course she does!" returned the vintner, indignantly ; "it is that that gives her her beautiful complexion."

"Well," said the blacksmith, whether she drinks ale or whether she doesn't, she asked us to drink, like a true lady, as she is."

"She didn't ask me," remarked Tom ; "his lordship ordered me a pint of rhubub."

"That was to prevent your catching the cholera after the gooseberries," explained Dick. "Why, they say you devoured ten quarts!"

"Oh! I'm sure I didn't!" answered Tom, reproachfully. I ain't so greedy as that comes to. If I ate six or seven, it's as much as I did."

"Ah! but how many peaches?"

"Not more than three dozen and a half."

"Ho! ho! ho!" laughed everybody.

"There was one I bolted whole, when the gardener bawled at me. It was that that disagreed with me ; but I'm all right now!" and smiling upon the surrounding company, he took another dip into the ale.

"Take care, Tom," said one of the bystanders. "You know you can't stand it ; take care of your head."

"But I know I can stand on my head!" spluttered Tom, upon whose silly brains the liquor was taking effect.

"No, he can't!" cried mischievous Dick, edging him on to a trial of his skill. "He can't stand on his head!"

"I'll show you!" exclaimed Tom, bending down in a preparatory manner.

"Oh! on the ground," interposed Dick, in a tone of assumed scorn. "Any fool can stand on his head on the ground; the difficulty is to stand on your head on a stool," winking aside to the crowd as he spoke.

"One's as easy as the other, every bit!" cried Tom, and mounting on a bench, he put down his head, grasped the edges with his hands, threw his legs boldly up in the air, and fell with a crash on his back, amidst the laughter of the spectators.

"Oh! my goodness gracious!" said Tom, as they lifted him up. "That was a bang, wasn't it?"

"You don't call that standing on your head, do you?" inquired Harry, laughing.

"No!" replied Tom, shrugging his shoulders; "I call that falling on my back. Where's the ale?"

Retiring with his companions to one of the

tables, he continued eating and drinking as vigorously as ever.

In the meantime, amongst the townspeople Lady Godiva's promise was freely canvassed.

"How thinkest thou?" said one of a group to his neighbour; "will her ladyship hold good to her word?"

"No doubt of it," answered the person addressed; "did she not promise, and would a pious lady as she is break her word?"

"Not willingly; but her modesty might take alarm, or the earl might withdraw his consent at the last moment, might he not?" asked the first speaker.

"If he does he forfeits his word, and she will still claim the right to our exemption from this tax."

"Undoubtedly!" exclaimed all.

"Then, whether she rides or whether she does not," said Ironbrace, "let us drink her health, as the noblest lady in the land."

The toast was responded to heartily on every side, and again the empty tankards required replenishing.

At this juncture three personages, walking at a sauntering pace, appeared in the market-place, approaching in the direction of the inn.

Their attire, unlike that of the citizens, rendered them particularly conspicuous.

They were clad in well-worn loose shirts that had once been dark-blue, but which, by the combined efforts of time, the sun's rays, rain, and dust, seemed to have arrived at a kind of neutral tint that had no particular designation.

These were confined at the waist by broad leather belts with brass buckles, and reaching half way down the thigh, revealed rather full breeches of faded crimson cloth, which appeared to form part of their under-garments, the arms of which, and what could be seen of their vests, being of the same colour and material.

Their legs were bound with leathern thongs, commencing from their shoes, and fastened below the knee.

Gloves with strong gauntlet tops, broad-brimmed hats, and large cloaks with jagged and tattered edges that appeared to have seen much service, completed their apparel, whilst in their belts might have been seen three formidable long two-edged daggers.

Their careless, lounging walk, and the indifferent manner in which they jostled anyone who chanced to stand in their way, suggested their belonging to a class partaking more of the bully or the ruffian than the peaceful citizen or traveller.

They belonged, in fact, to a body of Dutch mercenaries known by the title of *Brabançons* or Cottereaux, an importation from Brabant, a city of the Netherlands.

These brigands, or whatever they might have been justly called, had served in large numbers under the deceased king when engaged in his wars with his rebellious barons, and being now disbanded, they wandered to and fro, ostensibly as soldiers, but uniting all the qualities of highway robbers and marauders, with the additional qualification of being always ready to perform any piece of villany if they were paid for it.

Their tanned and sunburnt features contrasted with their light hair, which fell straight over their shoulders, and their fierce moustaches put the finishing touch to portraits anything but prepossessing.

They were dusty, as though they had travelled far, and appeared struck at the unusual throng of people in the market-place.

Bungs, the landlord, had found it necessary, from the influx of customers and the increased demand for ale, to bring out a large table as a temporary resting-place for the bottles, cups, and tankards brought into requisition.

This conspicuous object, laden with its goodly array of foaming flagons, caught the eyes of the three thirsty travellers, who, with the cool *nonchalance* that seemed to characterize all their motions, swaggered up to the table just at the moment when the health of the Lady Godiva had been drank, and a fresh supply of strong ale had refilled the tankards.

The tallest, and apparently the strongest, of the three unceremoniously seized upon the largest flagon within his reach, and having taken a deep draught, passed it to his companions, who rapidly finished it.

Now it so happened that Tom, who, in his anxiety to melt the golden piece the earl had bestowed upon him, was drinking as much as he possibly could himself, and treating everybody else, had a few moments before magnanimously ordered all the cups on the table to be refilled at his expense, consequently the liquor the Brabançons swallowed was Tom's property.

Tom was, as usual, laughing and eating gingerbread, and did not observe the robbery, but quick-eyed Dick did; and, seeing a chance of a little more recreation at Tom's expense, called his attention by giving him a dig in the ribs.

"Oh!" said Tom, wincing, and turning round immediately; "what's the matter?"

"Did you see that fellow there?" said Dick, in a low voice, pointing to the Brabançon.

"What fellow?" asked Tom in a somewhat indistinct voice, looking intently at nothing.

"That German-looking vagabond with the light hair and moustache," answered his informer, directing his attention in the proper direction.

"Y-es," replied Tom, "I think I see something."

"He's been drinking your ale," said Dick.

"Oh, has he?" answered Tom; "that's all right; I hope he liked it."

"Hope he liked it?" cried Dick, in well-feigned surprise; "you mustn't allow yourself to be taken liberties with in that manner."

"Mustn't I?" said Tom, innocently, looking at his adviser very wisely, and discovering that he had four eyes and two heads.

"Certainly not."

"What am I to do?"

"Go and ask him what he means by it."

Tom, having got the Brabançon by a great effort within the range of his vision, started to approach him, which he did with some difficulty; and, having done so, grasped his cloak for the double purpose of arresting his attention and steadying himself.

The Dutchman turned sharply round and looked at Tom.

"What d'ye want?" he said, angrily.

"I wants to know," answered Tom, "whether

you knows whose ale you've been a pourin' down that throttle of yourn ?"

" I neither know nor care," said the Brabançon, scornfully.

" Don't you ?" answered Tom ; "then let me tell you," he continued, placing his two hands on his hips, and looking up winking and blinking in the face of the Dutchman, "it was my ale."

" Indeed ! then let me tell *thee* that this throttle of mine has room for three times the quantity it has already received," replied the cool customer.

" You've got a tidy swaller of your own, then," said Tom ; "but I paid for that ale."

" I never pay," remarked the Brabançon, coolly.

" Tell him he must pay for your ale," whispered Dick in his ear.

" You must pay for my ale," said Tom, obediently.

" I pay ?" echoed the ruffian, with a hoarse laugh ; "ha ! ha ! Pooh !"

" He says, ' Pooh," remarked Tom, turning to his mischievous friend.

" Lay hold of him, and tell him he *must* pay," directed Dick.

Tom accordingly turned once more to the Dutchman, and in order to be sure of his man, grasped him by the throat.

" It's no use your sayin' ' Pooh !' you *must* pay !" exclaimed Tom.

The Dutchman, who towered above Tom, looked down derisively upon his round face, and, taking a deliberate aim, spat in his eye.

This was too much for Tom's patience, and, seizing the first tankard that came to hand, he discharged its contents full in the face of his insulter.

" As you're so fond o' drinkin' other people's ale, take that, Mr. Longlegs," he cried.

The Brabançon, astonished, enraged, and saturated with ale, that half-blinded him, seized the daring Tom, and would have shaken all the gingerbread he had eaten into his boots, had not his friends interposed.

" Come, Mr. Foreigner," cried Dick and Harry, backed up by Will and Joe, " fair play's a jewel. You drank his ale, and have a right to pay."

The Dutchman replied by a sound something between an oath and a growl, and seemed to be intent upon demolishing the hapless Tom, when the boys, springing upon their friend's back in a body, pulled him away by main force, and so suddenly that they all rolled on the ground together, whilst at the same moment the strong arm of Ironbrace was extended with its panoply of muscles and sinews in front of the savage Dutchman.

" If you wish to try your strength," said he, with a grim smile, " try it upon this, not on that half-brained fool there."

The two mercenaries, seeing a prospect of a quarrel, interposed on behalf of their companion.

" Come, come," cried one of them, " do you English, who boast of hospitality, take offence on a day of rejoicing such as this appears to be, because a stranger, weary and thirsty, drinks accidentally from the wrong tankard ?"

" Oh !" said Tom, who had risen from the ground, " if it was an accident "——

" Of course it was an accident," replied the other. " Besides, if we have emptied your cup, can we not re-fill it ?"

This unanswerable argument completely satisfied Tom, and the three strangers became on tolerable terms with the surrounding company, and drank like fishes at Tom's expense, who was delighted, and in the fulness of his heart proposed that one of them should marry his granny, and come and live in their cottage, but as there was some difficulty in disposing of the other two, this idea was dropped.

Lady Godiva again became the subject of conversation.

" 'Twill be a rare sight for us all when she rides round the town," cried some.

" She is so very beautiful !" said others.

" Oh, marry come up !" exclaimed some of the wives of the revellers, who were waiting for their husbands, and who were a little inclined to be jealous at the warm admiration evinced by their spouses for Lady Godiva.

" Methinks," remarked one of these invidious females, " beautiful and pious as this saintly dame may be, she lacketh somewhat of modesty in thus exposing herself."

" Thou art ungenerous, wife," said the husband of the speaker ; " dost thou not know it is for all our sakes she consents to take this step ?"

" How do you know that, under cover of seeking our benefit, she doth not undertake this to gratify her own vanity ?" replied the ungenerous one.

" Oh, yes," chimed in another ; " she is proud of her handsome shape, and desirous, like any common wench, that all the city should see it."

" Then be assured that none of the city will see it," said a young man who had sat quiet and unobserved at a corner of the table listening to the conversation, and who now rose and came forward.

" Not see it ?" cried everybody. " What is to prevent them ?"

" The sense of honour and right that lies in the heart of every Englishman."

All eyes were turned upon the stranger who uttered this reproving and at the same time flattering speech.

He could in age scarcely have numbered more than seventeen years, being in appearance a mere light-limbed stripling ; his light brown hair fell in natural waves over his shoulders, whilst a clear blue eye of singularly sweet expression lighted up a face that would have been almost feminine in its beauty, had it not been counteracted by the occasional gleam of power that appeared in his features, and the composed dignity of his attitude, as he confronted the babbling assembly.

All felt, without knowing why, they stood in the presence of a superior ; whilst he, as he stood before them in his plain, modest, though not poor attire, looked like the spirit of wisdom and beauty enforcing the claims of virtue.

There was a pause ; every tongue was mute.

"The noble Lady Godiva," continued the young stranger, " is about to make a great sacrifice for your sakes ; would it not be a fitting return for such a sacrifice, if, instead of every window and gateway being crowded with gazers, one and all, throughout the whole length and breadth of the city, voluntarily kept sacredly within doors, and turned away their faces until she has made the circuit of the city ? "

There was another pause ; such a thought had not appealed to them before ; the young stranger's words impressed them.

" Would it not," he went on, " be a scandal and disgrace to us all if the glance of even one licentious eye should bring a blush to that pure cheek as she passes on her way ? I ask you, would it not ? "

" The youth is right," said an old gray-haired man, " and we will heed his council. Say you not so, friends ? "

" Yes, yes ! " cried a score of voices, " we will keep within doors ; and more than that, we will issue a proclamation to that effect."

" D'ye hear that, Tom ? " said Dick, to his simple friend.

" Yes, I hear," said Tom, " and I mean to say it's a shame ; I should ha' liked to have had a peep."

He pressed forward as he spoke ; the ale he had drank had made him obstinate.

" Look'ee here, good people ! " he cried.

Everybody wondered what was coming.

" It's very well known to all on us," Tom continued, " that Lady Godiva's—hic—hair is uncommon fine, an'—hic—uncommon long, an' when she lets it—hic—loose, it comes down to her—hic—heels, and covers her like a—hic—veil, so that look as long as you like, my boys, you wouldn't see the least—hic—bit on her ; there never was such hair in the world, an' never will be, as—hic—Lady Godiva's hair."

Having delivered this oration, Tom staggered to a seat, missed it, and sat down on the ground, smiling as usual, and in his own mind as happy as a king—probably a great deal happier.

The Dutchman stalked forward ; he had been drinking ale furiously, and he had not forgotten the drenching he had received at Tom's hands ; he advanced to where Tom was sitting, and looking down upon him, exclaimed emphatically—

" It's a lie ! I, Karl of Brabant, say it's a lie ! "

CHAPTER V.

THE DUTCHMAN CHALLENGES TOM TO A BOUT AT CUDGEL-PLAYING—TOM ASTONISHES THE DUTCHMAN—THE TWO-EDGED DAGGER—THE STRANGER RESCUES TOM—THE MOB HANG UP THE DUTCHMAN.

PEEPING TOM, who distinctly heard this repeated assertion, looked round vaguely to discover the speaker.

" Who said it's a—hic—lie ? " he inquired, blandly, looking everywhere but in the right direction.

" I did ! " again exclaimed Karl, sternly.

" Oh, did you ? " said Tom, raising his eyes, and fancying he caught a glimpse of the Dutchman somewhere in the clouds ; " then just give us a—hic—hand up, will yer ? "

The Brabançon replied by lifting him roughly on to his feet.

Tom staggered against him. " I suppose," he said, " if I tell a lie I'm a—hic—liar, eh ? "

" Decidedly."

" You means to say as there's a woman in the world as has got longer—hic—hair than—hic—Lady Godiva ? "

" I do," said the Dutchman. " There's a woman in Brabant whose hair trails three yards on the ground."

" Ho ! ho !—hic—ho ! " roared Tom ; " you're a thinkin 'of a horse's tail, not of a woman's hair."

At this sally all the bystanders laughed, to the great irritation of the Dutchman, who dared not, on account of the number of the tailor's friends, make an open show of hostility ; he therefore adopted an expedient, which he thought promised him at least an opportunity to revenge himself without appearing to do so.

" I'll play you a bout with cudgels, my friend," said Karl, in a friendly way, to Tom ; " and he who first draws blood shall receive his opponent's apology, with the right to hold to his own opinion."

" Oh, won't I ! " said Tom, eagerly ; " if there's one thing I should—hic—like to do, it would be to—hic—chip his crown who don't know the difference between horse-hair and—hic—woman's hair."

The coming trial of skill was received with loud acclamations.

Tom was quickly stripped of his doublet by his companions, whom he privately informed that he did not intend to kill the Dutchman quite, and received his cudgel with the dignity of one from whom something was expected by his fellow-townsmen.

The Brabançon, on the other hand, coolly poised the weapon between his finger and thumb for an instant, and then, twirling it in the air, brought it down with a sharp " whish " for the purpose of testing its weight.

" Form a ring," cried Oxgall, the butcher.

This was immediately accomplished, and the combatants entered the arena and faced each other.

The Brabançon, half closing his eyes, peered out from beneath his light but thick brows upon his antagonist.

Tom, who was as full of ale as an untapped barrel, by dint of shutting one eye and tightly screwing up one side of his face, which looked like a full-moon convulsed, contrived after much effort to get as distinct a view as possible of his foe, who at one moment appeared to be a long way off, and the next unpleasantly near, to say nothing of two heads that were continually moving from side to side, and puzzling him at which he should strike.

" I wish he'd hold his head still and not keep dodgin' about in that way, then I might have a chance o' givin' it a crack," thought Tom, who stood, as usual, with his toes turned in and looking as unlike a champion as could possibly be imagined.

" Go it, Tom ! " " Mind your nob ! " " Look out for your knuckles ! " " Cover your brain-pan ! " and such like suggestions were kindly thrown in by the boys.

The Dutchman did not appear at his ease, and looked at Tom with a puzzled air, as though there was something connected with him he could not comprehend.

Ironbrace, who was watching him, understood the cause of this ; Tom was left-handed.

" It bothers the foreigner, that left hand of Tom's," he whispered to Oxgall, the butcher.

" All the better," he answered ; " it's lucky for him he is left-handed."

" Set 'em going," said Chipper.

"Are you ready?" asked Ironbrace.

"Yes," answered the Brabançon.

"Hic—yes," said Tom.

"Play!" cried the blacksmith.

The combatants made several feints.

Both had been drinking freely, and were in consequence less skilful, though probably more reckless.

As for Tom, who knew as much about the science of cudgel-playing as he knew about Euclid or algebra, he would not at that moment have quailed before King Richard himself.

"I hope to goodness he'll hit me on the head," he said to himself, "and then—hic—I shall be all right."

He hopped about the ring like a jackdaw, exposing himself in every possible way to his antagonist's blows.

Presently the Dutchman's cudgel descended with considerable impetus on Tom's head.

Tom simply sneezed and grinned.

"Ee! ee! ee!—hic," he said; "one to you."

No blood followed, so they continued.

Tom received three more blows on his invulnerable part, the head, and eventually one on his right elbow, that particular spot facetiously denominated the funny-bone.

It might have been funny to the lookers-on, but it had the effect of making the heroic Tom feel extremely sick; however, he mastered his sensations, and twirling his cudgel at random in imitation of his opponent, he suddenly dropped in such a thoroughly unscientific and new-fashioned blow, that he baffled the Dutchman's guard, and laid open one side of his face from the eye to the corner of the mouth.

A loud shout of applause hailed this feat.

The wounded ruffian was furious.

"Hell's curses!" he shouted, "I'll make you pay for that, you left-handed, botching idiot!" And rushing fiercely upon Tom, who was in a state of open-mouthed wonder at his success, he grasped him by the throat, and throwing him violently across his knee, he drew the formidable two-edged dagger from his belt, and in another instant the luckless Tom would have fallen a victim to the ruffian's fury, when his wrist was suddenly grasped by the young stranger, who, with a vigorous wrench his youth and the slight contour of his figure scarcely promised, disarmed the mercenary, and giving him a severe cross-buttock, laid him, half stunned and breathless, in the dust.

The whole occurrence had passed so rapidly that the bystanders seemed to awake as from a dream or reverie.

As soon, however, as they realized the imminent peril from which poor Tom had been preserved, their gratitude to the young deliverer, and their indignation at the cowardly act of vengeance contemplated by the Brabançon, were at once displayed.

A score of hands eagerly pressed those of the brave youth, and as many arms embraced him with genuine warmth, whilst the Dutchman's carcase was spurned by indignant heels, and loaded with execrations.

"Cowardly assassin!" "Accursed bandit!" "*Maudit* Cottereau!" burst from the indignant multitude.

"Hang the varlet by the heels!" cried one of the crowd.

"Ay, ay! Hang him! hang him!" flew from mouth to mouth.

"Who'll hang him?" interposed his two companions, in a bullying, blustering tone.

"We will," shouted Ironbrace, in a voice hoarse with drink and rage; "and you too if you dare utter a word or lift a finger to prevent us."

A rope was thrown into the ring, a slip-knot was quickly tied at one end and passed round the ancle of the prostrate ruffian, who was dragged unceremoniously to the door of the inn by the boys and Tom, who enjoyed the treat.

There one end was thrown over the sign-board, and the other, being seized by all who could get a chance of clutching it, the Dutchman in an instant was swinging in the air, and left dangling with his head downwards in spite of the ravings of his companions, who swore it was murder.

"Murder or not," said Ironbrace, "let him hang there till all the blood in his body rushes into his saffron cheeks, or a fit of apoplexy carries him off."

It seemed very probable that some such fate would have befallen him, had not the young champion who had disarmed him advanced.

"Release him, friends," he cried, "at my request; let us prove our contempt for his cowardice by letting him go free."

There was considerable opposition to this proposal by the crowd, but the youth had something in his manner that commanded acquiescence to his wishes, and in a few moments the rope was slackened, and the Brabançon allowed to come down with a run to the ground.

His companions raised him, and with looks that boded bitter and revengeful feelings, led him away, muttering oaths in their native language, and dire threats of vengeance against Tom and his preserver.

No sooner were they gone than the eyes of the crowd sought for the brave young stranger, to whom they longed to express their thanks, not only in words but in something more substantial.

Tom also was on thorns to treat him, but the stranger was nowhere to be found.

The twilight had drawn on, and been speedily followed by the night.

The curfew had sounded its warning note, and every mansion and cottage tenanted by our Saxon forefathers was hushed in darkness and silence.

CHAPTER VI.

THE MORNING APPOINTED FOR LADY GODIVA'S RIDE—TOM RESOLVES TO HAVE A PEEP—HE HIDES IN A HOLLOW TREE—HIS ADVENTURE THEREIN—HE IS EVENTUALLY RESCUED, AND GETS A DUCKING.

THE morning on which the Lady Godiva was to take her memorable ride, out of pure love and good-will to the people of Coventry, came in bright and beautiful.

At early dawn Lady Godiva, attended by her maidens, knelt before the altar of St. Osbury's Monastery.

Mass was performed, and the pious lady prayed that no dark scandal might attach itself to the act she was about to perform with so pure an intention of benefiting others.

As she rose from her knees the morning sun poured its beams through the magnificent stained glass window, bathing in a flood of gorgeous light the lovely devotee, and appearing like a glorious assurance that her prayer was heard and answered.

About the same time, our inquisitive friend Tom—who, I am sorry to say, had been carried home the night before drunk and incapable, to the great consternation of his granny, who believed in physic, and who dosed him with about half-a-pint of that favourite family medicine, salts and senna, and in spite of his express desire to be allowed to stand on his head all night, and his chivalrous offer to the horrified old lady to come out in the back garden and fight her, at last managed to get him to bed—rose from his slumbers.

His sensations, as may be imagined, were none of the pleasantest, being a compound of ale and salts and senna.

He went downstairs quietly, and going to the well, drew a bucket of cool water from its depths, and placing it against the wall, stood on his head in the pail, to the great amusement of Tinker, the dog, who thought a new species of tree had sprung up in the night.

After this operation he felt better.

He returned to the cottage, and after demolishing half a meat pie and drinking a quart of milk, sneaked out of the gate.

Tom could not master his inquisitive disposition, and in spite of the advice of the young stranger, the resolution of the whole town, and the proclamation that had been issued, that "*during the period of Lady Godiva's journey through the town no one should be seen out of doors, or even at their windows, under pain of severe punishment*,"—in spite of all these preventives he resolved to have a peep.

"I wouldn't miss sich a plummy sight for all the gingerbread in the world," he said to himself.

He accordingly hastened to a spot out of the town, where he knew the countess in the routine of her journey must pass.

It was a very retired locality, hard by the ruins of an old convent that had been destroyed by the Danes in the time of the Heptarchy.

Here stood a tree, which, though verdant and leafy externally, was hollow at the core, and as it happened, the cavity faced the road, and was partially concealed by the overhanging branches.

Tom gazed at this with great satisfaction.

"That hole was made o' purpose for me!" he exclaimed, snapping his fingers with delight.

Oh! wicked Tom!

He clambered up and looked in.

"Oh! ain't it jolly inside," he ejaculated. "I think I'll come an' live here. Wouldn't it be fun?"

He contrived to squeeze his fat body through the opening in the trunk, and was soon concealed at the bottom of the tree.

"This is splendid," cried Tom in an ecstasy, plumping himself down, but starting up again like a "Jack-in-the-box," as a fierce howl rung in his ears.

He had disturbed the slumbers of a ravenous old fox, and almost crushed it into the bargain.

The animal, thus at bay in the narrow limits of the tree, opened its formidable jaws, and with swelling tail and fiery eyes glared and growled at poor Tom, who thought his last hour was come.

"Oh! oh! oh!" he yelled, "I shall be gobbled up alive, I knows I shall! Oh! oh! oh!"

The fox, however, happened to be as frightened of Tom as Tom was of the fox, although neither was aware of the fact, and as Tom dodged round, he uncovered a small hole at the back of the tree, through which the fox had entered, and at which outlet he now made a rush, and escaped —all but his tail, at which the valiant Tom made a determined grab.

In vain the fox howled and tugged and spit; Tom held on as tight as wax.

"Here's a lark!" he cried; "fox 'untin' now! I must have this 'ere tail," he said, chuckling; "it'll do for granny to dust the room with."

So saying, he contrived to draw out his pocket knife, which he opened with his teeth.

"Now then, Mr. Fox," he exclaimed. And, with one slash, off came the tail, and away flew the fox with a terrific howl minus his brush.

Tom was delighted at his triumph.

"It's all right now!" he ejaculated. And, placing his trophy by his side, he began to wonder how long it would be before Lady Godiva appeared.

It was not, however, quite so right as Tom imagined.

His friends, the boys, knowing his prying disposition, and suspecting the result, had assembled early, and keeping out of sight, had watched him leave the cottage, and promised themselves an immense fund of amusement from what was to follow.

Little thinking how many mischievous eyes were upon him, Tom had ensconced himself in the tree.

Dick, Harry, Bill, Joe, and about half-a-dozen more adventurous spirits followed as quietly as so many mice.

They heard the disturbance in the tree, and saw the departure of the fox without his tail just as they were about to knock him on the head; the loss of his brush, therefore, saved his life.

The boys gathered round the tree.

All seemed very quiet—rather *too* quiet.

They wondered what was the matter.

"The fox can't have devoured him," said Harry.

They listened intently.

A deep snore announced the fact that Peeping Tom was asleep.

This was a satisfaction, at all events.

Dick mounted on Harry's shoulders, and looked in.

Sure enough there was Tom snoring away with his mouth wide open to his heart's content.

Dick descended, and they held a consultation.

They felt that Tom was decidedly in the wrong, and resolved to punish him.

But *how* was the question.

"What shall we do with him?" they inquired one of another.

"Let's duck him," kindly suggested Harry.

"Oh, that's not half enough," replied Dick; "we'll funk him out first, and duck him afterwards."

This appeared to give great satisfaction.

Bill and Joe were accordingly despatched to the town, where they borrowed a small brazier from Spout the tinker, a plank, hammer, and nails from Chipper, and from Poppyhead, the apothecary, they purchased several rolls of brimstone and a lump of *asafœtida*, a drug of a horribly filthy odour.

"Are you going to poison the whole town ?" said Poppyhead, as he served them.

"Oh, no," said Joe, "we're only going to smoke out a rat."

They lost no time in returning to the tree with the brazier full of lighted coals and the delicious perfumes they had purchased.

"Bravo !" cried Dick, "this will do." And, mounting upon Harry's shoulders, he, with as little noise as possible, nailed the plank across the opening in the trunk to prevent Tom's escape, who, in the meantime, slumbered on unconsciously.

All now being ready they crushed the sulphur, and having mingled it with the *assafœtida*, they turned the mass into a small iron shovel, heated over the brazier, and cautiously inserted it in the opening at the back of the tree.

"Oh! oh !" exclaimed the boys, holding their noses as they caught a whiff of the horrible effluvia, but ready to burst with laughter at the same time; "if it's anything like this outside, what must it be inside ? Won't Tom enjoy it."

Tom, whose head had dropped on one side, just over the shovel, and whose mouth was open, had the full benefit of the nauseous vapour.

He was dreaming of gingerbread. He seemed to be in his dream devouring large quantities of the delicious compound ; but suddenly he fancied the pleasant flavour become less agreeable, and gradually grew so abominably filthy, that he could stand it no longer. He awoke to find himself in a thick, suffocating vapour, and surrounded by the horrible odour that seemed to reign everywhere.

"Oh, dear ! oh, lor ! whatever can it be ?" he cried. "Ough! ough! ough!" he coughed. "I shall be chok—— Ough! ough! ough! Murd—— ough ! ough ! Oh ! what a 'orrid—ough ! ough ! —stink ! "

With desperate haste he mounted to where he expected to find the hole, but to his horror found it fastened.

"Oh! oh! oh !" he groaned in despair, as he let go, and fell to the bottom, overpowered with the abounding odours. "Oh ! oh ! what a wicked—ough ! ough ! ough!—boy I am ! Oh ! this is all along o' my—ough ! ough !—peepin' perpensities—ough ! ough ! I shall be choked, an' granny'll—ough ! ough !—wonder what's become o' me ;" and having gasped out this miserable confession, he lay groaning and blubbering, until Dick, thinking he had had nearly enough of that particular punishment, removed the plank, and looked in.

"What, Tom," he cried, "is that you ? "

"Yes, it *is* me," answered Tom, ruefully, "an' I'm almost pisoned with this ere awful stench. Give us a drink o' water. I'm a chokin' as fast as I can."

"All right," said Dick; "we must get you out first."

"Here's a rope," cried Harry. "Slip that under your arms, and we'll draw you up."

The rope, which had a noose at one end, was thrown in, and Tom, who only saw a prospect of being lifted easily out, passed it under his arms.

"All right," he cried, as soon as this arrangement was effected.

"Fire away, then," shouted Dick.

All the boys *fired away*—that is, they put all hands to the rope, and up flew poor fat Tom, and stuck tight in the opening in the trunk.

"Oh ! oh ! oh !" roared Tom ; "you're a scrunchin' of me !"

"Pull away, my boys !" shouted remorseless Dick. "Yeo-ho!—yeo-ho !" they bawled, sailor-fashion, tugging at the rope with all their might, and laughing fit to split their sides.

"Oh ! oh !" yelled Tom. "Oh ! my bowels ! you're pullin' me in half ! "

"Now, then ; one good one all together !" cried Dick, and with a last united effort, out flew Tom with a bang.

He pitched on his head, and stood so for a second, like a nine-pin the wrong end upwards, and then rolled over on his back.

"Water ! water !" he cried.

"Poor fellow !" exclaimed Dick, with mock commiseration ; "he must want some water. Let's take him to the pond."

"Yes," gasped Tom, rolling his head from side to side, and lolling out his tongue like a Polar bear in the dog days, "Take us to the pond, that's good fellers."

Tom was hoisted from the ground, and hurried off to a pond not far distant, on the brink of which a tree reared its trunk, a straggling branch of which hung conveniently over the water.

Here they placed Tom on the ground, who was innocently unconscious of the treat in store for him.

They had seated him with his back to the water, whilst Harry, taking the rope in his hand, hastily climbed the tree, and passing it over the trunk, descended, drawing the end with him.

"Now then," cried Dick, " here's the water."

"What a blessing !" ejaculated Tom, smacking his dry lips.

"Are you fond of tadpoles ?" inquired Harry, considerately.

"I don't mind if it's full of tadpoles," said Tom, earnestly ; " only just put me so that I can get at it."

"We'll oblige you in a minute," cried Dick, whose exertions to subdue his risible faculties were considerable. Turning to his companions, he said, in a low voice, "Lay hold of the rope."

The injunction was eagerly complied with.

"Water ! water !" exclaimed Tom. " I am so dry."

"Go !" enjoined Dick.

The boys ran out, as boys might naturally be expected to run under such circumstances, and away flew inquisitive Tom Winker, to his great astonishment and horror, to find himself dangling over the weedy surface of the stagnant pool.

"Oh! oh !" cried Tom ; " I can't get at the water here."

"Of course you can't," said mischievous Dick. " It isn't to be expected you could—is it, boys ? Let him get at the water ; it's so dreadful to be thirsty."

He gave a signal to the boys—an expressive one—brief, but comprehensive, " Drop him.'

The rope was instantly slackened, and the un-

LADY GODIVA;

OR, PEEPING TOM OF COVENTRY.

THE APPARITION.

happy victim was simultaneously floundering in the middle of the pond, gasping, struggling, kicking, and ejaculating, and at every attempt sucking in more than he required of the nauseous draught and the slimy green scum that floated on the surface.

The frogs and tadpoles, with which the pool abounded, were in a state of frantic excitement, and scudded hither and thither, in all directions, to avoid the terrible monster who, they doubtless imagined, had come to devour them.

After Tom, according to Dick's judgment, had had enough water to quench his thirst, he was hauled up for a few moments to drain, and also to feed the sight of his friends with his highly picturesque appearance, which—as he was.

No. 3.

covered from head to foot, face included, with green weed—somewhat resembled a dissipated sea monster who had been making a night of it.

"Ugh!—ah!—oh!—oo—oo!" he gasped.

"What *does* he look like?" roared Dick.

"Neptune in a fit!" cried Harry.

"A pickled porpoise!" shouted Bill.

"Baron Slimy!" said Joe.

"Duke Duckweed!" suggested somebody else.

"Ha! ha! ha!" screamed the whole band of juveniles.

"Let me down!" bawled Tom, who was evidently with excitement, tadpoles, and weeds, more out of his senses than ever, and didn't know what he was talking about.

"Let him down, poor fellow!" said Dick.

The rope slackened once more, and Tom had a second edition of the pool.

"Oh!—oh! I shall be drowned," he cried.

"Swim! Swim!" shouted his tormentors.

"I—I—can't!" spluttered Tom.

He was wrong.

He couldn't sink, he was too fat.

"Strike out with your arms and legs, Tom!" counselled the boys.

Tom struck out frantically, but from some peculiarity in the manner of performing this operation his head disappeared immediately beneath the surface, and his two fat legs, with the toes turned in as usual, stuck up in the air.

"Ha! ha!" roared the young torturers, "he's diving. Look at him! Hold on tight, Tommy, and sing out when you get to the bottom."

But poor Tom was in that peculiar position when singing (the singing in his ears excepted) was utterly out of the question.

He began to think he had paid for peeping, and got his receipt in full—or rather in mouthsful.

He indulged in a somewhat hasty and confused recollection of his last cake of gingerbread, his old granny, and the dog Tinker—all jumbled up together with mud and duckweed, and, ejaculating mentally, not orally, "I'm a bustin'!" quietly made up his mind to be drowned.

But this was by no means the intention of his young friends, who only wished to teach him a lesson.

Accordingly, when they saw the striking out become less vigorous, they slung the rope from over the end of the branch and hauled Tom ashore.

Not a great deal too soon, inasmuch as a few moments more would have converted a practical joke into a deep tragedy.

Tom lay quietly on his back, with his toes turned in, and swelled up, from the quantity of water he had swallowed, to such an extent, that Dick gave it as his decided opinion that "something ought to be done" immediately.

Something accordingly was done immediately, and that something was that Tom was stuck upright on his head until the opinion prevailed that the water he had swallowed had drained out of him.

He was then released, and allowed to fall on his back, and the draining process having been attended with favourable results, Tom shortly after gave signs of reanimation. He sneezed several times, opened one eye, shut it, and opened

the other, and finally opened both, and declared himself much better, to the great consolation of the boys, who delighted in Tom though they played him so many tricks.

"Lift me up," he cried. "I've had enough to drink. I think something to eat 'ud do me good. Let's go home to breakfast."

"Come on, then," said Dick and Harry, hoisting him on to his feet by a jerk under his arms. They were a little too premature, so was Tom, who had swallowed several tadpoles and a few infantine frogs.

When he was set upon his legs he looked round somewhat vacantly upon his facetious comates, curled up the corners of his mouth into a very peculiar species of grin, swayed to and fro for a moment, and then quietly collapsed and sat down again.

"What's to be done?" asked Dick.

"He wants shaking up," suggested Harry.

"We'll shake him, then," joined in the rest.

They were about to carry this resolution into effect, but in the meantime Tom had fallen back on the grass, and was fast asleep.

This being the case, they pulled down some branches from the trees, and with this formed a temporary kind of bier.

On this they placed the sleeper, and each by turns lending their assistance, they carried him home to his old granny, who had missed him, and was in a state of great agitation, being fully persuaded that he had wandered from his sleeping apartment, and fallen down the well.

At the old dame's request, they conveyed him upstairs to bed, and the door being locked, he was left to sleep off the effects of his morning's adventures; whilst his granny occupied her faculties in cleaning his garments from the mud and weeds that clung to them, and in emptying his pockets of the frogs and tadpoles that had found their way there.

CHAPTER VII.

LADY GODIVA'S RIDE—THE PLOT TO INTERCEPT HER—AWFUL FATE OF THE BRABANCON—THE ASSAULT—TIMELY ARRIVAL OF THE YOUNG STRANGER—THE ASSASSINATION PREVENTED—SUDDEN APPEARANCE OF THE SKELETON MONK.

AND now the hour drew near when the Lady Godiva was to start on her famous expedition—that was to be in future times recorded in the annals of history.

The clocks had proclaimed the hour of nine as Lady Godiva, attended by her maidens, proceeded to the tiring-room of the convent, wherein the officiating priest was wont to assume and put off his sacred vestments, and there, by the fair hands of the young girls who waited on her, her lovely form was divested of its usual covering, and she stood in their midst in all her naked, unadorned loveliness.

At ten the bells of the market church rang a lively peal, and this being taken up by the other religious edifices throughout the district was to be the appointed signal for all who wished well to the town, and looked for heaven's blessings on their labours, to close their shops and draw the curtains of their windows, that the noble lady might suffer no shame from the bold eye of public gaze.

As the last tones of the bells were fading upon the ear, the small arched door leading from the chamber to the exterior opened, and there, tethered to a ring in the wall, beneath which was a stepping stone, for the convenience of equestrians, stood the favourite steed of the Countess, Lilly, pawing the ground, and champing his bit somewhat impatiently.

The Lady Godiva uttered a few kind words to the noble animal, that elicited a low neigh of recognition.

Placing her foot upon the stepping stone, and grasping his flowing mane with her hand, she vaulted lightly into the saddle, where she sat with the ease and grace of a perfect horsewoman.

Lilly, as though conscious of the precious burden he was carrying, walked slowly, but proudly away, whilst she, as she sat with her magnificent hair falling around her, looked like a beautiful statue shrouded in a veil of golden threads, through which the dazzling whiteness of her marble skin, like the dim outline of some entrancing vision, could be indistinctly seen.

As she passed through the town the streets were deserted. Neither male nor female, old or young, rich or poor, were to be seen.

The silence was unbroken, save by the echo of the horse's hoofs, and but for the bright morning sun that made the face of nature radiant and beautiful, it might have been dead midnight.

Onward and onward, slowly but surely, went the noble steed.

As she rode along, her heart was lifted up in grateful aspirations that the minds of the people had been, with one accord, disposed to observe this general retirement.

She had made the circuit of the town, and was now on the road to the Convent of Saint Osburg.

On her way back, she had to pass the ruins of an old monastery, that had been built and destroyed by the Danes during the Heptarchy.

Only a comparatively small portion of this ancient edifice remained. The long grass grew thick and rank in its ruined cloisters, and flourished around and over the tombs where the monks of yore slept silently, whilst the clustering ivy and the creeping foliage clung to the crumbling arches, and, stirred by the night breeze, fluttered to and fro in the pale moonlight, forming fantastic shadows on the grey flags beneath.

This ghostly relic of the past went by the name of "Grey Monks' Ruin," and in those dark and superstitious times was supposed to be haunted by spectres, the most conspicuous of which was declared to be a gaunt grey figure, in a cloak and cowl, which covering shrouded, so said report, the ghastly form of a *skeleton*.

Few people passed near the ruin after dark without shuddering, and muttering a *Pater noster*, and hardly one could have been found daring enough to have entered its mouldered and time-worn precincts.

Some there were, however, who were not impressed with these superstitious terrors, since at this time the ruin was tenanted by four individuals.

Three of these might have been recognised at once as the Brabançon who had, a few days before, made themselves conspicuous in the market-place, and who were now in their present locality as the hired instruments of the fourth, a dark-browed, swarthy, powerful man, whose bearing and attire proved him of a rank superior to the rest, from whom he kept apart; and, wrapped in his ample cloak, reclined upon a flat, moss-covered tombstone, apparently lost in thought.

This was Othniel, Lord Raven, who, with his breast filled with unholy desires, and his memory at war with his conscience, was waiting the flight of a few brief moments to add another crime to his already burdened catalogue.

He would have been handsome had not the fierce glance of his eye and the strongly indented lines upon his face bespoke a life passed in the indulgence of sensual gratification and stormy passions, which had left their withering stamp upon his features with unmistakeable distinctness.

Why, as he reclined upon that old tomb, were his brows knit in a dark frown? and why did he press his hand upon his forehead, and clench his lips together, as though to shut out some intruding thought, or check some angry exclamation?

Why, as he took from his breast a locket, and fixed his burning gaze upon a lock of golden hair contained therein, did the quick blood rush into his dark face, rendering it darker still?

Several causes helped to produce these effects.

He remembered the time when he had turned traitor to his brother; when that brother was, by his perjury, falsely accused of treason to his king, his estates forfeited, and he banished from his country a ruined exile, whilst he himself—the despoiler—inherited the rich domains, as the price of his perfidy.

Then there passed through his mind the tormenting vision of the violet eyes and golden tresses of a lovely girl he had once madly loved, but whose heart he had failed to impress, and whom he had seen snatched from him by a rival.

As he gazed upon the lock of hair which, when she was a mere girl he had severed from the fair Godiva's golden tresses, the past seemed to come bitterly before him.

"Fifteen years," he murmured, "since we met; since, with her sweet, blue eyes calmly looking into mine, and her golden locks perfuming the breeze as it passed by them, she told me she had given her heart to Leofric of Mercia, my school-fellow and brother soldier. I bore it then," he continued bitterly, "for I had neither power nor wealth. Now I have both, and I am here to see whether fifteen years have dimmed the lustre of her eye, or destroyed the lovely symmetry of her body. The charms she denied me once may have decayed, but if not, if she be still beautiful as of yore, like a second Tarquin will I swoop upon my prey, that no power shall keep from me."

Othniel had come over from Yorkshire, where his estate was situated, under the ostensible pretext of paying his old schoolmate a visit of courtesy, but in reality to see his wife, Godiva, whose beauty had so powerfully impressed him almost twenty years before.

He was on his way to the castle, when he was informed of the resolution she had taken, and resolved to delay his visit, and, couched in secret, feast his eyes upon the charms of the woman he loved in all their unveiled beauty.

Nor was this all. One evil thought had given birth to another, until, in the recklessness of his headstrong passions, he resolved to seize her, and in defiance of all honour, right, and morality, force her from her home and the husband she loved to his own domains, although he was himself married.

For this purpose he selected the haunted ruin as his place of action.

He knew there were vaults beneath, that would offer a secure asylum, where none would dare to penetrate, whilst he himself, intent upon the success of his projects, laughed at the superstitions of the time, and defied the skeleton monk and his host of spectres.

Of the peril that awaited her, the beautiful Godiva was utterly unconscious.

With her heart full of pure and kindly thoughts that shone in her features, and, as it were, spiritualised her beauty, she rode calmly on.

As she drew towards the "Grey Monks' Ruin," the sky became overcast, a bright flash of lightning shot across the heavens, followed by a peal of thunder.

"Curses on it!" muttered the profane Othniel; "we are going to have a storm, and her onward progress will be arrested. Go out, one of you fellows," he cried, to the mercenaries, "and see if there are any signs of her approach."

"I'll go," said Karl, who, in spite of his gashed and swollen cheek, was anxious to obtain a view of the naked beauty.

"Bah!" exclaimed Rodolph, in a tone of disgust, "I wouldn't go a yard out of my way for fifty such sights. I had one wife, and, judging the rest of her sex by her, I set them down as a bad lot altogether."

"I don't," answered Karl, as he emerged from the ruin and proceeded cautiously down the road.

As he reached the tree, which had been the scene of Tom's previous adventures, the sound of horse's hoofs fell upon his ear.

He immediately placed a small whistle to his lips, and blew a sharp, shrill note.

His companions in the ruin started to their feet, and put on their masks; whilst Othniel pulled the hood of his cloak over his face so as entirely to shroud his features, nothing being visible but his eyes, that glared like two fiery meteors from two apertures cut for the purpose.

Karl, having sounded the whistle, mounted the tree and concealed himself in the hollow of the trunk.

"That was the signal agreed upon," said Rodolph. "The lady is coming. When she arrives here, what are we to do?"

"Await my commands," answered Othniel, sternly. "If the prize be still worth securing, you will rush forth at my signal, arrest the progress of the horse, and, snatching the lady from its back, convey her at once to the vaults beneath. You will find me there awaiting you. Be prompt in what you do, and cover her mouth, that her cries be not heard. Do not stir till I give the word 'advance!'"

At this moment the lightning again blazed through the ruin, and a hollow peal of thunder murmured over their heads, whilst a deep voice, that seemed to come from the depths of the earth, exclaimed, in solemn tones—

"*Man of unholy thoughts, beware!*"

Othniel started, and looked round.

"Who spoke?" he said, placing his hand upon his sword.

No answer was returned but the echo.

"Psha!" he exclaimed; "it must have been fancy!"

The beautiful Godiva was now approaching the tree.

The sky had grown darker, and the flashings of lightning and peals of thunder followed each other in rapid succession.

The concealed ruffian looked, gloatingly, from his hiding place upon the fair form approaching.

"Donder and blitzen!" ejaculated the profane Karl, taking his oath from the state of the elements, "she is lovely!"

The words had scarcely passed his lips when a vivid flash of lightning illumined the scene with a bluish glare, accompanied by a deafening peal of thunder.

The electric fluid struck the hollow tree, shivering it into a thousand splinters; and, simultaneously, a fearful shriek rose from the lips of the miserable Karl, who fell lifeless amid the smoking timber—a blackened, lifeless mass!

The horse on which Lady Godiva rode, alarmed at the lightning, trembled in every limb, and became restive and almost unmanageable, so that she did not observe the retribution inflicted on the Brabançon; but, urging on the terrified animal, she neared the ruin, when, as she passed its ruinous shadow, two masked men rushed out, and seized the horse by the bridle.

Horrified, bewildered, and ready to sink with shame, the beautiful countess veiled her blushing face with her hand.

"Why do you stop me thus, with sacrilegious hands, in the performance of this act of charity?" she exclaimed.

"We stop you because we're paid to do so," answered Rodolph, "and we must trouble you to dismount."

"You may kill me here where I sit, shameless ruffian as thou art," cried the beautiful countess, crimson with shame and agitation, whilst the tears started to her eyes; "but I will not dismount."

"I should be sorry," said Rodolph, "to leave the mark of my fingers upon your dainty skin; but my orders are imperative, and if you refuse to descend from the horse's back quietly I must employ a little gentle force."

"You will not—you cannot be so lost to manly dignity as to insult me thus!" cried the countess, the tears of indignant womanhood trickling down her cheeks; "or, if you are, heaven itself will interfere in my behalf. Oh, now do I see," she exclaimed, raising her beautiful eyes to the sky above her head, the inten tion of these sweeping tresses; they were not sent to foster pride, but, to shield me from the rude and unhallowed gaze of violent and wicked men."

"You're complimentary, fair dame, but I have no time to listen to your homilies," said Rodolph. "As I told you, I am not doing this on my own account. Handsome as you are, you might have ridden till doom's-day before I should have stopped you; but what must be, must be; so come on. Don't be alarmed, I won't look."

As he spoke, the mercenary, who was growing a little out of patience, grasped her wrist. The very touch of the man seemed to carry with it pollution, and the countess screamed aloud—

"Help! help me, merciful heaven! Help me!"

At the same time she threw her arms round the neck of the horse, to which she clung with desperate tenacity, in spite of the struggles and plungings of the animal, who was startled at the masked figures.

"Teifel!" cried Rodolph, angrily, "this is child's play. Come, madam, off with you!" and, holding the bridle with one hand, he essayed to clasp the waist of the countess with the other.

A shrill cry rose from her lips, as, releasing her hand for a moment from its grasp of the horse, she thrust the Brabançon back with a force that violent indignation could alone supply.

He staggered a few steps, and the horse reared; but before he could recover his hold of the bridle, his attention was attracted by an angry voice that shouted in his ears—

"Miscreant! Ruffian! Dastard! hold your polluting hand!"

The Brabançon had barely time to draw his sword and turn in the direction of the voice, when he encountered the fiery glance of the young stranger of the market-place, who, with a sweeping head blow, beat down Rodolph's guard, and inflicted a gash in his forehead that stretched him senseless. His companion, thinking that the new comer rather too formidable an antagonist under the circumstances, released the horse and decamped.

Lady Godiva glanced for an instant at her preserver, and again veiled her fair face in her hands.

"Lady," cried the youth, who studiously averted his face from the countess, "take no shame I beseech you at my presence here; rather regard it as a special interposition of Providence in your behalf. I take heaven to witness that these eyes of mine have not even glanced at you, neither shall they. I would have them rather plucked from my head than that they should bring a blush to the cheek of one so pure and good."

"I believe you, young sir," replied the countess, "and I thank you, as the instrument under heaven of preserving the honour of Godiva and Leofric of Mercia. I can pay you no higher compliment than in saying I feel secure under your protection."

The youth's cheek glowed with pleasure.

"But do not remain here, good sir," she continued. "I have nothing to fear for the rest of the journey; but for your generous interference in my behalf, receive my warmest thanks, and be assured it will not prove ungrateful. Accept this ring." Holding towards him as she spoke a valuable amethyst, which he received without turning his head towards her. "And, if it be in my power to serve you, show me that ring, and it will be the pledge that that power shall be exercised in your behalf."

The youth bowed, with averted face, in reply.

"What is your name?" she asked.

"I am called Eric," was the reply.

"Eric," replied the countess. "I shall remember that name to the end of my life; and you, I prophecy, will not regret the hour when you saved from insult and outrage the Lady Godiva. Farewell!"

During the latter portion of the foregoing dialogue, Eric, occupied with his own thoughts, had not observed the gradual approach of a masked figure, who, by a slight circuit, (rendered necessary by the young man keeping his gaze turned away from the Lady Godiva), had gradually approached him from behind.

The moment the horse began to move away, Eric stood rooted to the spot, with his eyes fixed thoughtfully upon the ground.

The masked figure approached.

It was Othniel, who, seeing Rodolph stretched upon the ground, and missing Johann, his companion, who had fled, divined Eric's work in the frustration of his plans, and thirsted for vengeance.

He accordingly drew near—a feat which, owing to Eric's abstraction, was exceedingly easy to perform, and as the young man stood still and statue-like, wrapped in a deep reverie, the villain approached unseen and unremarked. He drew from the folds of his cloak a long sharp poniard, and raised it aloft. The keen blade flashed for a moment in the sun's rays, and in another instant would have been buried in the youth's back, when, suddenly, an arrow, shot by an unseen hand, pierced the palm of the hand that grasped the deadly weapon, which fell to the ground.

Uttering a cry of pain, Othniel desperately broke the arrow short off near the wound, and drew it out; and then, rushing from the spot, disappeared amidst the ruins, almost before Eric had recovered from his surprise.

Without pausing an instant, Othniel mounted his horse that was grazing in the ruined cloister.

"Who, in the fiend's name, fired that arrow?" he exclaimed, through his teeth, that were clenched together with pain.

"I did!" answered a solemn voice at his side.

He turned in the direction of the sound; and there, in the shadow of a gloomy porch, stood, leaning upon his bow, the ghastly form of the SKELETON MONK.

CHAPTER VIII.

THE GREY RECLUSE—PROCESSION BY TORCH-LIGHT—HOW PEEPING TOM GOT OUT OF HIS SICK-ROOM—HOW HIS GRANNY GOT INTO THE PIG STYE.

OTHNIEL uttered a cry of horror as this terrible object met his gaze; and, driving his spurs deep into his horse's flank, fled like lightning from the spot.

Not that fear was the principal cause of his haste ; he had an end to gain.

The dazzling beauty of the Lady Godiva had fired his evil passions, and he resolved never to rest till he had secured her.

It was, therefore, his policy not to be known in association with the late unknightly and dishonourable attempt.

From the three instruments he had employed he had nothing to fear ; one was dead, and the other two were strangers to him, he having met them casually on his journey, and, finding them ready to perform any act for money's sake, had employed them to seize upon the person of the Lady Godiva.

This plan, however, being frustrated, he resolved to exercise more patience and to proceed with caution.

Eric, having recovered from his surprise, followed the masked figure who had evidently attempted his life, taking with him the poniard the assassin had dropped.

He searched the ruin, but in vain ; Othniel having departed before he arrived there.

He had just ended his search and was about to depart from the place, when he was encountered by a man of a dignified and noble countenance, with long, flowing grey hair and beard, enveloped in a long grey hooded cloak.

"Ah ! Father Ambrose," he cried : "my life has been attempted, and preserved by some unknown hand."

" I know it," replied Ambrose.

"The assassin entered these ruins, and he "——

" Has fled ; I know *that* too."

" Who could have fired the arrow that saved my life ?" remarked Eric, thoughtfully.

The old man took a bow from a recess in the porch, and, with a smile, held it up before the youth.

"I understand," said Eric ; " it was you."

" It was."

" I knew not that you were skilled in the use of the bow," exclaimed the youth in evident surprise, as he pressed the old man's hand with grateful warmth between his own.

" Have I not taught you to use a sword, Eric ? Why, then, should you be surprised that I am an archer as well as a swordsman ?" inquired Ambrose.

" I am not so much surprised, only that I have never heard you mention it," returned Eric. " But you say you saw the assassin ?"

" Yes."

" Did you know him ?"

" He was too closely disguised to render recognition possible," answered Ambrose.

" Your arrow compelled him to drop his dagger. I shall keep it as a memento of his good intentions," said Eric, producing the poniard he had picked up.

The old man glanced at it, and his face turned pale, but he concealed his emotion.

" It is a formidable weapon," he remarked. " I must teach you the use of the dagger."

" 'Twould have been as well, if you had sent an arrow whizzing after that masked assassin, I think," said Eric.

" My son," replied the old man, " there are some crimes whose punishment is best left in the hands of heaven. Its retribution, though often tardy and long delayed, is nevertheless inevitable and certain. It is so with this man ; his hour is not yet come. Let us return to the cave."

And, leaning on the shoulder of the youth, the old man quitted the ruin.

They proceeded to the spot where the body of Rodolph had been lying a few moments before, but it had disappeared.

There were great rejoicings in the city of Coventry, when it was publicly announced by the trumpeter and crier that the Lady Godiva having fulfilled the conditions of her compact, the odious tax was revoked.

The whole town indulged in festivities.

Bonfires were lighted, and, to crown the whole, there was a grand procession by torchlight, in which the beautiful Lady Godiva rode through the town on her white horse, Lily, to receive the congratulations of the grateful people.

The noble steed, white as milk, and richly caparisoned with crimson and gold trappings, was led by a young page. On its back was mounted the Lady Godiva, gorgeously attired in a riding habit of green velvet, trimmed with ermine, that set off to the greatest advantage her magnificent and queenly figure.

Her splendid golden hair, which had been the theme of many a wandering troubadour, was knotted up behind, and then suffered to fall loosely down her back, being fastened by a plain gold band encircling her forehead ; in the centre of which was a magnificent emerald, that glittered in harmony with her dress.

The procession was headed by a body of torchbearers ; these were followed by a band of trumpeters. Next came two spearsmen, bearing polished shields, that glittered gorgeously in the torch-light ; and after these, the Lady Godiva on her white steed.

Behind her were a fresh body of torch-bearers and spearsmen ; and, in the rear of all, the archers and guards of the earl.

As the procession wound its way through the town, the flashing and glittering of the torches, the martial sound of the trumpets, the joyous pealing of the bells, and the enthusiastic cheer of the multitude, together with the majesty and beauty of the countess, and the martial splendour of the guard that accompanied her, formed a scene of joy and beauty that those who witnessed it never forgot.

Our old friend, Peeping Tom, with his dear friends, the boys, was in his glory on that night, and had wound himself up to a state of gingerbread and ale that was wonderful to behold.

It may be supposed that their enjoyment was unusually intense, from the circumstance that it was with the utmost difficulty Tom was enabled to get out at all.

If the truth must be told, the prolonged soaking he had in the pond had been rather too much even for his constitution, and he had been confined to his bed for several days.

Poppyhead, the apothecary had been sent for, and had declared the symptoms to be highly inflammatory ; the consequence was that Tom had been ordered blisters and gruel, to his great disgust.

His old granny, now that she had him under lock and key, was in her glory; she fastened up the window, and kept the bed-room door locked constantly.

It was quite useless Dick or Harry, Bill or Joe, showing themselves at the door, and requesting to be allowed to see *dear Tom*—the only answer they could get out of the old woman was that "*dear Tom* was at death's door, and must not be disturbed."

What was to be done? The boys were quite at a loss without Tom; there was no fun without him. They called a council of war.

It was the night before that on which Lady Godiva was to ride through the town by torchlight.

"We must have him out *then*," said Dick.

"Certainly," said Harry.

Bill and Joe and the whole body echoed their opinion.

"How's he to be got out? that's the question," inquired Dick. "His old granny says he's at death's door."

"Oh, bother his old granny! What does she know about it? The idea of Tom's dying! He'll never die," suggested Harry."

"What shall we do?"

"Well, first of all, I don't believe he's a bit more ill than any of us at this moment," remarked Dick.

Everyone believed the same.

"Well, then, now comes the point. How *is* he to be got out? Because he must be got out somehow."

"Yes, yes, of course."

"Stick a lump of gingerbread on a clothes prop, and show it him through the window; that'll bring him out, if anything will."

"But the old woman's nailed up the window."

"Set fire to the house!" cried one enthusiast.

"Tie a string across in front of the door, give a good rap, and when the old woman comes out she'll pitch on her nose, and we can all bolt in in a body, burst open the bed-room, and lug him out by main force," was another suggestion.

None of these, however, seemed to be exactly the thing.

Suddenly Dick proposed that they should watch the opportunity when the old dame went out to market, and by dint of mounting upon one another's shoulders, have a personal interview with Tom through the bedroom window.

Accordingly, no sooner had old granny departed, after carefully locking up all the doors and cupboards, and knocking several extra nails into the window, than the boys proceeded to the garden at the back of the cottage, and endeavoured to attract Tom's attention.

"Bow, wow, wow!" barked Harry, in imitation of Tinker.

"Mol-row, ow, ow—oh, do come out!" plaintively uttered another, after the fashion of perambulating cats on the tiles.

"Is he asleep?" cried Dick. "Here, Joe, you're the tallest, just lend me your shoulder, will you?"

The shoulder being forthcoming, Dick mounted, but could not reach the window, which was still several feet above him. "We must try the ladder," he cried, jumping down.

There being no such article belonging to old granny, they managed to purloin one from the garden adjoining.

Tom, who had been asleep, was roused from a delightful dream of gingerbread, and opened his eyes just in time to see the top of a ladder appear at his window.

"Ullo!" said he to himself, "who's that? It can't be that sneakin' old granny o' mine comin' up the ladder to peep in an' see what I'm doin'!"

His surmises were soon dispelled by seeing the well-known features of Dare Devil Dick.

"It's Dick, I declare," cried Tom. "So it is!"

Immediately after Dick's voice was heard without, calling "Tom, Tom!"

"I'm 'ere," he cried, rolling himself out of bed, and waddling to the window.

"How are you, old fellow?" cried Dick. "Not dead yet, eh?"

"Dead? No!" answered Tom; "but I shall be before long, if granny doses me with much more o' that 'orrid gruel. Oh! I can't abear it!" he continued with a shudder. "'Ave yer got such a thing as a lump o' gingerbread in yer pocket, or a bit o' stick-jaw?"

"No," cried Dick, "but there's going to be a procession by torchlight and bonfires to-morrow night. Lady Godiva's going to ride round the town again."

"Lor, yer don't say so! Is she, though? Torches and *bungfires*, oh, my heye!" exclaimed Tom. "An' 'ere am I shut up like a mouse in a cage."

"You're well enough to come out, ain't you?" inquired Dick.

"Well enough!" cried Tom, in a tone of indignation. "I never wur better in my life; it was only the tadpoles as made me a little bilious for a day or two; but I'm as right as a trivet now."

"Then why don't you come out?" asked Dick.

"For a very good reason," answered Tom, "because I can't get out."

"Can't you open the window?"

"Open the winder? No! there's three ten-penny nails, a screw-driver, and two gimlets hammered into that to keep me from opening it. Granny's a tight fist, I can tell yer."

"Isn't there a chimney in the room?" inquired Dick, after a pause of reflection.

"Ah, the chimbley!" exclaimed Tom, suddenly, a ray of hope lighting up his features. "So there *is* a chimbley," and as he spoke, he went to it and looked up. "It'd be rather a tight fit I'm thinkin'," he said to himself, "but I can't stand this 'ere doctoring, so 'ere goes. I wouldn't miss the torches and the *bung-fires* for the world."

And having finished his soliloquy, he put his head up the chimney.

"Bravo!" cried Dick, who saw him from the other side of the window. "Are you coming?"

"I'm a goin' to try," bawled Tom, "but I can't see 'ow I'm to squeeze myself through that 'ere chimbley-pot at the top."

He disappeared up the chimney as he spoke, and Dick, descending by the ladder, informed the anxious tribe below that Tom's first attempt at escape from prison was in progress.

The ladder, all was forgotten in their anxiety to see Tom's round face once more, either bursting out at the side, or protruding at the top of the chimney-pot.

They listened anxiously.

Strange and muffled sounds were distinctly audible in the chimney.

"What's the matter, Tom?" cried several.

"Here somethink alive in the chimbley, with horns an' goggle eyes—old Nick, I think!" yelled Tom.

There was now a considerable quantity of fluttering and struggling, and then, from the top of the chimney, out flew a large horned owl; and, almost immediately afterwards, followed a nest and several smaller members of the same family, that rolled down the thatched roof into the hands of the delighted waiters below.

"Owls!" they cried simultaneously, and at the same instant Tinker, the dog, perhaps mistaking the precise meaning of the word "owls," and thinking it was in some way connected with another word of a somewhat similar sound, that reflected upon his own personal habits, began to howl most piteously.

"Hang the dog!" cried Dick, "he'll rouse the whole neighbourhood."

There being no rope near at hand, the capital punishment was not carried out, a slight hint merely that he had better shut up and go to bed, being given in the shape of a sharp pelting with any available articles nearest at hand, from pebbles to flower-pots, which had the effect of quieting the demonstrative animal, and leaving the juvenile conspirators at liberty to watch the progress of Tom's escape.

His voice was distinctly heard at the top of the chimney.

"I'm up at the top, an' nearly out," he cried; "but I can't get over the chimbley-pot, an' I'm stuck fast,"

"Go in a burster with your head, my boy," said Dick. "It's thick enough for anything."

"So I will," answered Tom, and immediately there was a volley of bumps fired at the chimney-pot from Tom's thick skull.

All the boys laughed heartily.

"That won't do," sang out Dick; "press upwards steadily, as hard as you can."

"I am a pressin' like old boots," cried Tom, speaking as a person would who was using violent corporeal exertion.

Very shortly a strange cracking sound was heard, and the next moment there was a different sound, as though something had given way, and out popped the upper part of Tom's person, with the chimney-pot tightly wedged on his head.

A shout of triumph greeted him.

"'Ere I am at last!" he cried; "better late than never."

Having extricated himself from his confining quarters, the ladder was placed so that he could put his foot upon it, and Tom, who was on all fours on the slanting roof, turned himself round and cautiously planted his foot upon the top rail.

"Now I'm all right!" he cried; but suddenly there was a cry of alarm raised.

"Your granny's coming!"

"Oh, bother my granny!" he exclaimed, dutifully.

There was no doubt about it.

Old Dame Winker was really coming, and to make matters worse the ladder was suddenly removed by some excited being (Dick Dare Devil, who kicked it away), and Tom as instantaneously found himself hanging on to the ridge of the roof with both hands, whilst the boys had made themselves invisible.

"Oh, goodee gracious me!" cried his granny, "what's he doing now with the chimbley-pot on his head?"

The old lady was suddenly impressed with the idea that he was light-headed, and had effected his escape by the chimney, as was indeed the fact.

Not having anything more effectual at hand to cool his distempered brain, she seized a bucket of water that stood near at hand, and dashed its contents over Tom, who held on like a barnacle to the ledge of the roof.

The sudden sousing caused him to relax his hold, and no sooner had he reached the ground than his worthy relative seized upon him with both hands, with the intent of transferring him once more to the placid retirement of his bed-chamber.

"Come along, Tommy dear; there, be a good boy," cried the old dame. "Come back to bed."

But *Tommy dear* didn't see it, and positively refused to do anything of the kind.

Old granny also was not to be done, and accordingly a friendly little maternal struggle took place, which ended in Dame Winker's sudden disappearance into the pigstye, which was the signal for a general shout of rejoicing from the boys, who, starting from their ambush, bore off Tom, sopping wet, in triumph to the market inn, where he was placed before the kitchen fire to dry.

At the end of half-an-hour he was sufficiently baked, and before the hour had expired was once more eating gingerbread and drinking ale with his young companions, with the promise of a bed at Dick's house to ensure his presence on the morrow.

And this was the manner in which Peeping Tom contrived to get a sight of the *Procession by Torchlight.*

CHAPTER IX.

THE YOUNG STRANGER VISITS THE CASTLE— LORD OTHNIEL IS SCARED BY A SIGHT OF HIS DAGGER—THE HERMIT REVEALS A SECRET TO ERIC, AND LEADS HIM TO HIS MOTHER'S GRAVE.

EARL LEOFRIC, disappointed of the money which he had calculated the tax would have secured him, by no means shared the general joy that pervaded the city.

His heart and soul were still fixed upon the crusaders, and he longed with irrepressible ardour to find himself at the head of his troops on the distant shores of Palestine.

The difficulty was, how to raise the necessary supplies?

LADY GODIVA;

OR, PEEPING TOM OF COVENTRY.

Scheme after scheme was thought of and abandoned, and the earl, in this state of mind, became moody and irritable, and paced up and down the courtyard with knitted brows and arms folded over his massive chest—the picture of discontent.

It was at this juncture that Othniel, his old acquaintance and fellow-soldier, arrived on a visit of courtesy, more to his surprise than pleasure.

However, as they had not met for many years, the earl smoothed his frowning brow, and prepared to give him a cordial welcome.

Lady Godiva received her former suitor with unembarrassed frankness and friendship.

She had not forgotten her rejection of his

offer, but considered that time would long since have healed any wound it might have occasioned.

She little knew how deeply he was implicated in the assault upon her modesty that had been inflicted a few weeks previously.

As for Leofric, he did not even know that Othniel had, in past years, been a suitor for the fair hand that he had snatched from him.

Great, therefore, was his joy when his old companion in arms offered to lend him twenty thousand marks, on condition that he should hold the castle and domains as security until the sum was paid.

This was at once agreed to by the earl, who, being now supplied with the necessary means, at once recovered his usual alacrity, and joyfully prepared for his departure.

Not that an involuntary sigh did not sometimes burst from his breast as he gazed upon the tearful eyes of his beautiful wife, as he reflected those tears were for his departure; but he controlled his emotion with the thought of the glorious cause in which he was to be engaged; and, as the chivalrous flame glowed in his breast, he forgot the sadness of parting in the bright prospect of a triumphant reunion with the fond wife he so tenderly loved.

It wanted but a few days of the time Leofric had determined upon to commence his march, when a message was brought to the earl that a youth desired an audience.

The message was accompanied by an amethyst ring.

He recognized the ornament at once as belonging to his wife, who, together with his friend, was present; and, turning to the former, he said, holding forth the ring—

"Godiva, do you know anything of this?"

"Yes;" she replied, the colour mounting to her fair brow at the thought of the peril from which Eric had rescued her. "The owner of this ring is the youth who preserved your wife from the assault of ruffianly violence. I pray you admit him."

"That will I, by the mass!" cried Leofric. "He is a brave youth, and deserves all kindness at my hands, and he shall have it. Bring the young man hither," he said to the messenger.

"This ring," added the countess, "is my pledge that the service he rendered me shall never be forgotten."

"Nor shall it!" exclaimed the earl, warmly.

At this moment Eric was introduced to the earl's presence.

The beauty of his person, and the symmetrical moulding of his figure delighted the earl, whilst on Othniel they seemed to have a more marked effect. His swarthy cheek grew paler, and the involuntary exclamation—"Heavens! how like!" broke from his lips.

His emotion was, however, unnoticed.

But it was not the mere personal beauty of the young man that so impressed the earl; it was the graceful ease and dignity with which a youth of not more than seventeen, clad in plain attire, stood unabashed and self-possessed, in the presence of rank and beauty.

"Welcome, young sir!" exclaimed the earl, in a genial tone, accompanying his words by a warm shake of the hand. "Right glad am I to have the opportunity of complimenting you upon your courage, and thanking you for the service you have rendered me in preserving my wife from insult."

The youth coloured with pleasure at these flattering words, and replied respectfully—

"I am more than repaid in having been the humble instrument of serving one so good and beautiful as the Lady Godiva, at the same time, I thank you, noble sir, for the praise you bestow upon my deeds."

The countess smiled and extended her hand, holding forth the ring she had given him.

"Receive back your pledge, my gallant knight," she said; "you must never part with that."

"I never will, lady," answered the youth kneeling to receive the jewelled ornament, and respectfully pressing the white hand that tendered it to his lips. "This is the first prize I have won in the lists of knight errantry, and I shall treasure it in memory of the giver, and as an earnest of future victories."

"You come as a suppliant, do you not?" asked the countess.

"Yes, lady," replied the youth.

"What is your name?" demanded the earl who had kept his eyes fixed admiringly upon the young man.

"Eric," answered his wife, anticipating his reply.

"Are your parents living?" again inquired the earl.

"No, my lord; I am an orphan," answered Eric, somewhat sadly.

"Poor youth!" murmured the countess to herself. "How proud might a mother be of such a son!"

"What would you of me?" asked the earl, after a slight pause. "What service can I render you?"

"I hear your lordship is about to depart for the crusades."

In mentioning that word, Eric had struck the chord more than any other harmonious to the earl's ear.

"I am," he cried, exultingly. "Can sword be drawn in a more religious cause, than against these infidel Saracens?"

"Impossible!" replied the young man with equal enthusiasm. "I long to enlist in this glorious cause. Humble as I am, I would fain strike a blow beneath the sacred banner on the shores of Palestine; it is for that I am here, to entreat your lordship to number me among your troops, that I may go with you; share your dangers; fight by your side!"

"Fight!" exclaimed the earl, glancing at his delicate though firmly knit limbs. "Art thou strong enough to endure the scorching blast of the desert, or to wield the crusader's sword?"

"Try me, my lord," boldly returned Eric.

The earl at once drew forth a ponderous double-edged sword from his side.

"Let me see you wield that," he cried.

Eric, with sparkling eyes, grasped the handle of the heavy weapon, and, like a second David preparing to decapitate a Goliah, he waved it thrice over his head, and then, allowing it to descend in sweeping strokes from right to left, and again from left to right, he dropped the point, and stood calmly resting upon the cross hilt.

A murmur of undisguised admiration burst from the lips of the earl at the performance of a feat the youth's appearance scarcely promised.

"By the mass!" he cried, "you have the strength of a young Hercules."

"I am indebted less to that than to skill for the ability to wield this sword," replied Eric, presenting the weapon to the earl, who replaced it by his side.

"And to whom are you indebted for that skill?" inquired Leofric; "the prowess of the pupil bespeaks a skilful master. Who taught thee to use the sword?"

"A hermit, called Ambrose; the same who brought me up. He has been a father to me," said Eric.

"Have you the permission to join these wars?"

"I have. It was he who counselled me to come hither. Say, my lord, may I enlist beneath the banner of the Earl of Mercia?"

"Yes, by heaven you may!" exclaimed the earl, heartily. "Proud shall I be to number among my brave volunteers one who unites in himself the attributes of Apollo and Hercules. Go, tell your guardian I accept your service gladly."

Eric bowed, and joyfully quitted the apartment.

He hastened to inform Father Ambrose of the success of his mission, whilst Othniel pondered darkly in his mind the likeness between the youth who had so lately stood before him and one to whom the finger of conscience pointed, as it whispered in his ears the stern accusation—

"*Thou hast destroyed thy brother!*"

Excusing himself to his host and hostess, he left the chamber and, throwing his cloak around him, quitted the castle, resolved upon gratifying his roused curiosity by questioning the youth who had just given such unmistakable proofs of superiority.

Eric — who had flown rather than ran or walked, in his eagerness to relate his interview with the earl to Father Ambrose—was far ahead on his way to Charn Wood—or, as it was called from the denseness of its foliage and the depth of its gloom, the Wood of Shadows—where, in a cavern hollowed by the hand of time, or formed by some bygone convulsion of nature, dwelt the solitary and mysterious man he sought.

Othniel shouted to him to stop.

The youth partially turned his head, but either not distinctly hearing the command, or not caring to obey it, continued his course.

"He hears, but will not comply, this warlike stripling," muttered Othniel, in whose breast even this slight incident was sufficient to kindle a feeling of anger.

A trooper at this moment passed him on his way to the castle.

"Lend me your horse, my good fellow," he cried to the soldier. "I wish to overtake yonder boy."

The man, who recognised the visitor of the earl, immediately dismounted, and Othniel took his place in the saddle.

"You must walk fast now if you can outstrip me, my mettlesome champion," he said to himself, as he galloped off.

He rapidly gained upon the youth, who, hear-ing the sound of horse's hoofs, turned without pausing in his walk to see who was coming.

"Stay!" shouted Othniel.

At this word Eric paused, and turned round to await the rider's approach.

"Why did you not stop when I called?" asked Othniel, in an angry tone. "If you think of being a soldier you will have to learn that obedience is a necessary attribute, and that you must obey the word of command."

"Only of my *own* captain," said Eric, who was nettled at the offensive manner of the new comer.

Lord Raven made no reply to this, beyond an impatient frown, and repeated the question.

"Why did you not stop?"

"I have stopped," answered Eric.

"Yes; but the first time I called?" continued Othniel.

"I did not hear you."

"Why, then, did you turn?"

"I remember now," replied Eric, "hearing a voice, but it was indistinct, and I thought it was fancy."

There was a simple truthfulness about this reply that appeared to satisfy the questioner.

"And now that I have stopped, what would you with me?" inquired Eric, "for I am in haste."

"Do you not remember me?" asked Othniel.

The young man, who had never removed his eyes from the speaker's face, replied—

"Were you not in the castle just now?"

"I was, and was struck with the ease with which you wielded the earl's weapon."

"'Tis nothing!" exclaimed the youth, carelessly.

"'Tis everything!" replied Lord Raven. "You must have been taught by an experienced swordsman to do what you have done."

"Perhaps I *have* been taught by such a one," answered Eric, with a quiet smile.

"I should like to see him," returned the other.

"He dislikes observation, and courts not the society of any one."

"He will not object to mine," said Othniel. "You are going to him now; I will accompany you."

"No!" answered the youth, firmly. "You remarked just now that to obey was a virtue in a soldier. I consider myself one now; and, in refusing to comply with your request, I am carrying out the principle of obedience."

"I do not *request*," exclaimed Othniel, sternly, "I *command!*"

"I do not acknowledge your authority!" returned the youth, firmly.

Lord Raven, grasping the edge of his cloak in his left hand, involuntarily smote his forehead with vexation, drawing his cloak up with the action.

As he did so, his face was shrouded by the drapery, which gave him an appearance so like that he had worn on the day he had sought to assassinate Eric at the Grey Monks' Ruin, that the latter recoiled with an involuntary exclamation—

"What is the matter, boy? Why do you start?" he cried, suspiciously.

Eric almost unconsciously had fastened his eyes upon the leathern glove that encased his lordship's right hand, as though he would have penetrated the covering."

Othniel's vindictive eye noticed this fixed glance, and he already hated the earnest gazer.

"Are you aware that you are—ignorantly, of course, but impertinently—insulting Lord Othniel Raven by this presumptuous scrutiny?"

A strange thrill, not of fear but anger, seemed to pass through the young man's frame at these words.

"Are you Lord Othniel Raven?" he inquired, still scrutinising the glove.

"I am. Why do you keep your eyes fixed upon the glove?" he asked, in a tone of subdued irritation.

"Because," continued the youth, deliberately, "if you are he whom you declare yourself to be, the hand that glove conceals should have its palm pierced by an arrow."

"How, dog?"

"And because," he added, in the same calm, but impressive tone, "if your name be Othniel Raven, this dagger belongs to you. Here are your initials on the haft."

As he uttered these words, he drew from his vest the poniard Othniel had dropped when the arrow had pierced his hand, and held it up before him.

Had a serpent stung the conscience-stricken assassin to the core of his heart, he could not have started more violently than at this simple act.

The horse he rode, constrained by the convulsive jerk of the bridle, went almost upon his haunches, and when he partially recovered from the shock, Eric had disappeared.

Father Ambrose sat in the entrance of the cavern, which, though the sun shone brilliantly in the heavens, was shrouded in twilight gloom. Eric shortly after arrived, with a countenance flushed with haste, and eyes sparkling with excitement.

"Your service is accepted?" said Ambrose, smiling.

"Yes, father," answered the youth, who frequently addressed the hermit by that title, and who then detailed minutely all that had passed from the moment when he entered the presence of the earl, up to that in which he sent Lord Othniel reeling back in his saddle at the sight of the dagger.

The old hermit heard him calmly, though a close observer might have traced various emotions in his changing features as Eric proceeded in his narrative. When he reached the culminating point of the dagger, a sad smile played upon his face.

"Give me the dagger," he said; "the weapon of an assassin should not be used in honourable warfare."

He received the dishonoured steel from Eric, and placed it carefully in a large chest in one of the recesses of the cave.

The intervening time flew rapidly by, and the night previous to Eric's departure had arrived. During the last few days the hermit's manner and bearing, always kind and gentle to the youth, had softened into almost womanly tenderness.

Often when unnoticed his eyes might have been seen eagerly fixed upon the boy, and only withdrawn to hide the tears that gathered there and blinded them.

It was a lovely night.

The moon shone in unclouded radiance upon the sleeping world, and penetrated wherever she could even the impervious recesses of Shadow Wood.

On that night the hermit, his arm thrown caressingly around the neck of Eric, took his way to a quiet glade in the forest.

Here they seated themselves on the spreading roots of a giant oak, and for a time each seemed too much occupied with his own reflections to be able to give them expression.

At length Ambrose broke the silence.

"You rejoice at the prospect of leaving this quiet sylvan abode, to mingle with the busy world, do you not?" he said. "Your young heart bounds with exultation at the stormy career before you, and even now yearns to exchange the calm silence of this peaceful wood for the din and carnage of the battle-field; is it not so?"

"I confess the change you speak of has a charm I cannot hardly account for even to myself," replied Eric. "There is only one thought that damps the bright prospect."

"And what is that?" asked Ambrose.

"Yourself, father," answered Eric, pressing the old man's hand affectionately; "what will you do when I am gone?"

"I shall exist by thinking of you. I shall picture you treading an honourable though a perilous path, in which my prayers, unceasingly offered, may help to guide you. This is, perhaps, the last night we may ever sit together as we do now, therefore let the words I utter sink deeply into your heart. You are not the poor, unknown, portionless being you appear; but one descended from a noble lineage—of noble birth."

The young man started up.

"Tell me my father's name?" he cried, eagerly.

"Not now," replied the hermit. "Treachery and slander have cast a blight upon his fair fame; but if there is justice in heaven's decrees, the time will come when your father's honour shall be restored. Till then, let not his son do aught to tarnish it."

"I will not—I will die first!" cried the youth, earnestly.

"I know it," said the old man, and rising from his seat he exclaimed, "Come with me."

He led the youth a short distance through the woods to a spot where the trees, being planted at wider intervals, allowed the moon's rays to fall to the earth.

Here he paused, and pointed to a small and narrow mound of earth, at the foot of a sycamore, on the back of which was rudely carved the inscription :—

"*In Memory of the Loved and Lost.*"

"There, Eric!" he exclaimed, in a tone of solemn sadness, "lies your mother!"

"My mother!" echoed the astonished youth.

"Yes," replied the hermit. "The ruin—your father's stronger frame was enabled to endure—fell with too stern a weight upon her gentle spirit. She died broken-hearted, and sleeps there in peace."

The youth knelt reverently over the lonely

grave that shrouded his mother's ashes, and the old man continued—

"You are now about to start upon the boisterous ocean of life's vicissitudes. Let truth and honour be your watchword; and courage, guided by mercy, your defence. And should aught tempt you to forget either of these noble attributes, let your thoughts fly back to this quiet resting-place, and remember that her spirit may be looking down upon you from beyond that moonlit sky."

The attitude of the old hermit, as he stood with his upraised hand pointing to the blue vault above, was solemn and patriarchal.

Eric rose from his knees, and threw his arms around the hermit's neck.

The old man and the young mingled their tears together.

"Tell me my father's name," at length cried Eric.

"Not now, my son," answered the hermit; "but take this," he added, placing a chain, to which was attached an antique cross, round the youth's neck; "and, should the chance of war, as most probably it will, ever bring thee to the presence of thy sovereign, show him this cross, and thou shalt see the issue. And now, my son, to rest, for the night is wearing, and thou must be stirring with the dawn to-morrow."

With these words they returned to the cavern, and in a short time Eric was wrapped in the last slumber he was destined to enjoy in his forest home.

CHAPTER X.

DEPARTURE OF EARL LEOFRIC TO JOIN THE CRUSADES—PEEPING TOM AND HIS FRIENDS BECOME INSPIRED WITH MILITARY ARDOUR —TOM RESOLVES TO BECOME A CRUSADER —HE LEVIES A FORCE TO GO TO PALESTINE, BUT GOES TO POT INSTEAD.

EVERYTHING was now prepared for Leofric's departure.

The day broke bright and cloudless on which, in a few hours, the earl was to behold the massive turrets of his magnificent castle becoming faded and indistinct in the distance.

Accompanied by his beautiful countess, the chivalrous nobleman attended mass for the last time in the chapel of the convent, and there, as the melodious choir sent up their sweet strains, causing the arched roof to echo with their harmony, the earl and his pious lady poured out their hearts in supplications that this expedition might be crowned with honour and success.

His troops, all fully equipped, were marshalled in grand array in the court-yard of the castle, where he was joined by several knights and squires, who volunteered to accompany him.

Eric was also there, with his sword buckled to his side, his young heart bounding with enthusiasm, as he listened to the shouts from the crowd assembled to see the earl's departure.

All being now in readiness, Leofric took an affectionate leave of his weeping countess. He solemnly recommended her and his daughter Algitha, who was then away, being educated at a convent in France, to the protection and knightly honour of Lord Othniel, and then,

gazing once more upon his proud domain and the spreading trees in the park surrounding it, he gave the word to march.

The shrill trumpets sounded, the banners fluttered in the breeze, and at the head of his troop, the brave earl, wearing the crusader's cloak, with the emblematic cross upon the shoulder, rode forward at the head of his forces amid the loud shouts of the multitude on his long and tedious journey, to meet the infidels on the scorching shores of Palestine.

Crowds of people, some on foot, some on horseback, and some in vehicles, followed the troops for a considerable distance from the town.

It is almost needless to state that Peeping Tom and his party were amongst the number.

Old Dame Winker had forgiven him for his forcible escape from his sick chamber, and given him permission to join the cavalcade, with the addition of a penny, to spend in gingerbread.

Tom, who knew everybody, had been, as usual, drinking ale and eating gingerbread to his heart's content, and as the trumpet sounded and the shouts of the crowd rang in his ears, he found himself inspired with an uncontrollable military ardour.

The boys had seized upon a small cart, and Tom had borrowed old Long Ears, his granny's donkey; so that they travelled in style.

Tom's breast glowed within him, and he would, at that moment, have given all the gingerbread he had in his pocket, to have met his old antagonist, the Brabançon, and have fought it out with him, there and then.

As it was, his excitement manifested itself in periodical gesticulations and ejaculations to the troops.

"Heads up, soldiers! Eyes right! Quick march!" burst from his lips at every convenient opportunity, to the amusement of some, and the disgust of others, who recommended him savagely to "Lie down," and "Go to bed," etc.

After marching six miles, the troops halted, and Tom and the boys, of course, halted too.

Tom was longing to get hold of someone who could give him some idea of the pleasures of a campaign.

At last he pitched upon a veteran, whose face, though hard and weather-beaten, was not deficient in kindly expression.

The old trooper stood leaning against his horse, chewing his moustache, and thinking how long it would be before he should see his wife and children again.

He was not smoking, that luxury not having been yet introduced into England.

"He looks a good-natured sort of an old chap, don't he?" said Tom to his friends.

They all agreed that he was full of the milk of human kindness, and urged Tom to speak to him.

"Go on," said Dick.

"Don't yer think he'll be offended?" asked Tom, dubiously.

"Oh, no," returned Dick. "Everybody knows you're rather soft in your upper story; so of course he can't be offended with you. Go on. Call him captain—he'll be flattered."

"So he will," said Tom, as he sidled towards the soldier, his companions watching him with great interest, and gradually drawing near.

The old trooper still chewed his moustache, and took no notice of anybody.

"How d'ye do?" remarked Tom, mildly.

The soldier glanced down at Tom's pancake face, gave a grim smile, and continued his meditations.

Tom suddenly recollected he had omitted the complimentary title suggested by Dick, and hastened to repair the omission.

"How d'ye do, *captain?*" he repeated, emphasizing the last word.

"Ha! ha!" said the trooper, firing off his monosyllables abruptly, and stopping short. "Captain! Ha! ha!"

"You *are* a captain, ain't you?" inquired artful Tom.

"You're a donkey!" was the blunt reply.

"No I ain't," answered Tom, innocently; "I'm Tom Winker; there's the donkey in the cart."

"Well, then," remarked the soldier, who was a wag in his way, "when you get in there'll be *two* donkeys—one inside and one out."

The boys, who were listening, laughed and nudged each other.

Tom smiled all over his face, and looked at them triumphantly over his shoulder, as much as to say, "See how well I'm getting on with this man."

"Have a bit o' gingerbread?" he continued, offering a piece to the trooper.

The man glanced at it; and, taking it, deliberately offered it to his horse, who immediately devoured it with great relish.

Tom was delighted.

"That's somethin' like a 'orse, to eat gingerbread!" he exclaimed, with enthusiasm. "If I'd a known he'd a liked it I'd a brought ever sich a lot."

"It's quite enough," said the soldier.

Tom, growing bolder, continued—

"I s'pose you've been in battle, hain't yer?"

"Battle! Ha! ha!" laughed the soldier, in his usual short, dry manner; "I've lived in it all my life."

The boys, at the mention of the word "battle," drew round.

"It must be very jolly to be in a battle," said Tom, unctuously. "What's it like, Mr. Captain?"

"Noise! Confusion! Blows! Bloodshed!" answered the trooper, emphatically.

"I s'pose yer gets a crack on the 'ead sometimes, doesn't yer?" asked Tom.

"Ha! ha!—look here!" as he spoke, the soldier removed his steel morion, and pointed to two deep scars upon his skull.

"Oh!" said Tom; "that'd just do for me. I shouldn't mind that."

"Wouldn't you?" returned the trooper, with a significant shake of the head. "Wait till you get it, and you'll see."

"Oh!" said Dick. "Tom doesn't mind how much his head's battered about: it's as hard as a brick, and there's nothing in it, is there, Tom?"

"I know there is," said Tom, grinning with the utmost complacency (he was proud of his thick head). "Granny says it be full o' mashed potatoes."

The trooper laughed at this, and the boys joined in chorus; but Tom laughed the loudest of all.

"I should like to go to the *kooorisades*," said he, seriously, when they had had their laugh out.

"The crusades, I suppose you mean?" remarked the trooper.

"Ah, yes; the crusades," repeated Tom, correcting himself; "an' 'ave a cross on my shoulder."

"Then why don't you go?" said the old soldier.

"Bothered if I don't, too!" said Tom, chivalrously. "An' you'll come, won't you?" he asked, turning to the boys. "We'll all go—eh?"

"Of course we will," cried they, nudging one another.

"You'll only have to show your face in Palestine," said the veteran, "and you'll frighten away all the Turks and infidels."

"I believe yer, I just will, too," cried Tom, proudly. "I'll astonish the *turkeys* an' the *fiddles*."

"Ha! ha! ha!" roared the boys.

"You can't go in that dress," said the trooper, who by this time saw through poor Tom's folly, and entered into the jest with the boys. "Where's your Templar's hat and cloak, with the crusader's cross on the shoulder?"

"Ah," replied Tom, thoughtfully, wondering whether there were any clean sheets in the drawers at home. "I shall have to get that, shan't I?"

"Of course you will," answered the soldier.

"Can you ride?" he inquired.

"Ride! I just can!" said Tom.

"Splendidly! On a broomstick," answered Dick.

"I can ride anything," continued Tom. "I hain't practised on our gate for nothin'."

"Let me see you mount my horse," said the veteran.

"Certainly," cried Tom: "I'll mount him. Give us a leg up, some un's," he called.

Dick and Harry hoisted him up immediately. Tom no sooner felt his foot on the stirrup bar, than he made such an energetic spring, that his foot shot out, and he came down with a run, flattening his nose against the side of the saddle.

"Oh, oh, oh, my nose!" he yelled.

"That won't do in battle," laughed the trooper.

"I can't a-bear knocks on my nose," said Tom.

"Never mind; try again."

The next attempt was more successful, so far as mounting was concerned, the only peculiarity about it being that Tom, who was always delightfully awkward, contrived to throw his leg over the horse's back, and descend into the saddle with his face to the animal's **tail**, which he grasped with great pertinacity.

"Bravo, Tom!" shouted the boys.

"This is somethin' like ridin', ain't it?" he said looking down with conscious pride.

"Where's the horse's head?" cried Dick.

"'Ow do I know?" said Tom. "I've got hold of 'is tail an' that's quite enough for me."

It was also a little too much for the horse, who became indignant, and commenced rearing and prancing, as the best expression of his feelings.

"Ain't this fine?" cried Tom.

"Splendid!" cried the boys, giving **at the** same moment a vociferous "hurrah!"

Up started the horse on his hind legs, and away flew Tom, all legs and wings, from his seat.

As usual he pitched on his head, and of course was, in consequence, none the worse for his fall.

He jumped up immediately, grinning from ear to ear.

"There," said he, "you see there's no frightenin' me."

"You'll do," remarked the soldier, laughing, "if you're good for nothing else, your head'll make a capital battering-ram."

At this moment the voice of the earl was heard.

Orders were given to march.

Again the trumpets sounded. Volunteers bade friends who had followed them a final farewell. The troops proceeded on their march, and the crowd returned, Tom Winker being fully resolved to equip himself as a crusader, and follow at the first opportunity.

Intent upon this step, Tom reached his granny's cottage.

Circumstances seemed propitious — Dame Winker had a visitor to tea.

"It's old Mother Trumper," said Tom, peeping cautiously through the door, which was partly open. "She's as deaf as a post, an' couldn't hear a cannon if it was fired off close to her, an' granny's obliged to bawl to make her hear, so atween the two we shall be all right."

They went round to the back door, and kept watch, while Tom, who, on condition of being the leader of the expedition, was to provide them with cloaks and helmets, cautiously ascended the stairs.

He soon arrived at an old oaken chest, where the good dame kept her linen.

The key was in the lock.

Tom turned it without a moment's hesitation, and glanced in eagerly at the snowy fabrics within.

Never before had he taken so much interest in such articles of clothing.

"'Ere's Templars' cloaks," he cried, enthusiastically.

In a few moments he had selected half-a-dozen sheets—the Dame's entire stock—and two night-dresses.

There being nothing else available, he left the rest untouched, and closed and re-locked the chest.

"Now, what shall I want next?" he said to himself, reflectively. "I know! I must have some *comparisons* for my donkey."

In search of this, he went into his granny's bedroom, and the first object that met his eye, was a bright-looking patchwork quilt, the old dame's pride.

"'Ere's the very thing!" he exclaimed, stripping it off the bed.

He then quietly descended the stairs, and having listened at the door as he passed, and assured himself that his old granny and Mrs. Trumper were bawling at one another across the tea-table at the top of their voices, he went out to his friends the boys, who awaited him anxiously.

"'Ere's six cloaks," he said, "an' two bed-gownds."

There was a general rush for the sheets, and in a few moments the whole party looked like a regiment of ghosts, as they stood with their white drapery thrown around them.

"What are we to do for helmets?" said Dick.

"I knows," answered Tom, after a moment's reflection."

He disappeared into the interior, and very shortly returned, laden with the whole stock of the dame's saucepans.

There was a general murmur of applause. They dared not shout, for fear of disturbing the old folks.

Tom, selecting the biggest, stuck it upon his head, with the handle hanging down behind.

His companions followed his example.

"The lids 'll do for shields," said Tom.

"So they will," cried the boys, each seizing a lid.

"But the black crosses on the shoulder?" remarked Harry.

"Ah," said Tom, with much concern depicted in his features, "the cloaks is nothink without the crosses, is they?"

"No, they *isn't*," answered Dick, with assumed seriousness.

"We'll 'ave the crosses," cried Tom, with a sudden idea. "The chimbley in the wash'us ain't been swep' for such a time; there's lot's o' soot there."

The smoky concretion was collected, and with this, crosses were smudged on to every shoulder, whilst with the same material they ornamented their upper lips with moustaches, and blacked their eyebrows.

This last operation gave general satisfaction. Each one looked at the other with admiration.

The last thing to be done was the caparisoning the donkey with the patchwork quilt, but this was the work of a moment.

All was at last completed.

Tom mounted Long Ears, shouldered a birch broom, and looked like—goodness knows what he did look like.

"Form a line!" shouted he, in the first burst of the pride of his heart.

The crusaders, who had laid hands on whatever implements came first in their way, in the shape of brooms, mops, rakes, and other miscellaneous articles, formed a line, and tumbled over each other, laughing in a very unmilitary and disorderly manner.

General Tom Winker was indignant.

"Now, just lookee 'ere," he cried, "if you means goin' to the *koorisades*, behave like *koorisaderses*, an' don't go a tumblin' over one another like that, an' dirtyin' the sheets. Attention!" he shouted.

"Why don't you attend?" cried Dick to Harry.

"Why don't you attend?" cried Harry to Joe.

"*Ordure* !' roared the indignant Tom.

Something struck him on his helmet, or rather on his saucepan. It was a potato.

"Who's that a chuckin' taturs?" he cried.

Something else immediately followed the potato; it was a turnip.

Tom's military indignation was at its highest pitch, and he could no longer endure this insubordination, and giving Long Ears two or three tremendous kicks in the ribs, he charged in amongst the rebels.

Occupied as he was with the double act of keeping his equilibrium, and flourishing his broom, he, of course, did little execution.

However, the boys pretended to be very much alarmed at his ferocity, and cried for quarter.

"Werry well," said Tom, "I forgives yer this once, but don't do it no more."

Peace being thus restored, Dick proposed that they should go round the town.

"So we will," eagerly exclaimed Tom. "Come on, single rank and file, an' I'll lead yer. Mind, no larks," he added, turning round to Dick, who was first in the ranks and armed with a pitchfork.

"Oh no, general," said Dick.

"Shoulder arms!" cried Tom.

The order was obeyed.

Dick, first giving the donkey several terrific progs with the pitchfork, shouldered his weapon.

Long Ears, who had his own private feelings, resented the puncturing he had received behind by kicking out violently.

"Wo ho! gently, old boy!" said Tom, grasping the pummel of the saddle.

Prog! prog! went the fork.

Kick! plunge! went Long Ears.

"Whatever is the matter with the hanimal?" cried Tom.

Prog went the fork again, and again the persecuted donkey became demonstrative.

"My goodness!" exclaimed the general, clutching the saddle, and righting himself. "'Ow he is a goin' on! I say," said he, turning round to Dick, who was "shouldering arms" in a most praiseworthy manner, as upright as a post, "yer ain't a doin' nothink to 'im, is yer?"

"No, I isn't," answered Dick, with the utmost sincerity. "He's only a little fresh, that's all."

"Oh! that's it, is it?" said Tom. "Then the sooner he gets stale the better I shall like it. We'll try again," he continued, settling himself in the saddle. "Now, then—all ready? Quick march! Hallo, boys!" he cried.

The boys halloed.

The pitchfork went to work—prog—prog—prog—the donkey kicked up his heels in the air—and Tom Winker, the gallant *koorisader*, was pitched head over heels once more on to his mother earth, the only difference being that this time he went over the head instead of the tail of his steed.

To complete the disaster, the gallant band, in their excitement, had forgotten their preliminary caution, and the consequence was, that when Dame Winker and old Mrs. Trumper, who had been talking incessantly for the last two hours, found it necessary to stop to take breath, it permitted the dame to become cognizant of the fact that there was a very unusual commotion in the back yard.

"Dearee me!" ejaculated the old lady, setting down her seventh cup of tea untasted. "Whatever can be the matter?"

In order to set her doubts at rest, she trotted off towards the garden, just as the command to "Hallo, boys!" had been delivered.

"It's Tom an' them boys up to their tricks!" cried the dame. "I'll teach them!" and, seizing her universal preceptor—a stout blackthorn crutched stick, which was also her companion in her pedestrian excursions—she opened the door.

The old lady was at first perfectly bewildered at the sight that presented itself.

Nearly a dozen boys, of various sorts and sizes, with saucepans on their heads, faces begrimed with soot, and wrapped up in sheets, howling like wild Indians, was enough to astonish anyone.

But that astonishment rapidly gave way to another sensation, as the truth flashed upon her that all this paraphernalia was her own private property.

Her eye fell upon Long Ears, the donkey, caparisoned in the patchwork quilt, and the prostrate Tom, who, entangled in his Templar cloak, and with the saucepan jammed firmly over his head, struggled in vain to release himself.

"My quilt! my saucepans! my brooms!" screamed the old lady. "Oh, you young willins!—oh, you warmint, Tom! An' theer's my sheets, too!" shrieked the horrified dame. "My beautiful clean sheets all tumbling about in the garden!"

Old Mrs. Trumper, who hobbled out to the door, and caught the last sentence very indistinctly, hobbled back again to the front, bawling out that the *Greeks were tumbling in Dame Winker's garden.*

In the meantime, the dame herself, who was a hearty old woman enough, had rushed amongst the crusaders, and by dint of strenuous exertions, and her blackthorn, snatching a sheet from one, and a saucepan from another, had recovered the whole of her property, though somewhat soiled and damaged.

The band of crusaders were put to flight, and she could now give her entire attention to the discomfited Tom, who, finding it impossible to get away, curled himself up quietly and lay still.

"Why, where's the boy's head?" cried the old dame, as she looked down upon him through her spectacles.

"In the pot!" moaned Tom, in a melancholy tone, "an' I can't get it out."

"It's a judgment upon yer, yer wicked boy!" exclaimed the dame severely; "an' now yer'll have to go about for the rest of your life with your head in a saucepan."

At this awful prospect, Tom's fortitude gave way, and he began to bellow.

"Oh, oh, oh!" he roared, piteously, "I shall never be able to eat nothing no more. I shall be starved! Oh, oh, oh!"

"Sarve yer right, too, yer disobedient, undootiful creetur!" continued the old lady, clutching the blackthorn ominously.

"No more gingerbread!" groaned the wretched Tom. "Oh, oh, oh!"

In the depth of his despair, he threw himself on his face and kicked.

Such an opportunity was not to be lost.

Down came the blackthorn with great effect, on the part which Tom had so kindly exposed.

Thwack—thwack—thwack! went the stick.

"Oh, oh, oh! O—o!" yelled Tom.

LADY GODIVA;

OR, PEEPING TOM OF COVENTRY.

RESCUED FROM DANGER.

"You'll dirty my clean sheets, will yer, eh?" cried the incensed dame, applying the stick. Thwack—thwack. "Yer'll take my quilt off my bed, will yer, eh?" Thwack—thwack. "Yer'll spile my saucepans, yer good for naught!" Thwack—thwack—thwack.

The old lady was by this time tired with her exertions, and now beginning to think her grandson had been sufficiently punished, and that his position, with his head jammed into a saucepan, was not altogether good for his health, shouted for assistance.

She was speedily answered by a body of neighbours, who came running, excited by old Mrs. Trumper's report, to see the *Tumbling Greeks in the garden*, but who, instead, found **Tom** and his granny in the relative positions just described.

After a little consultation, a couple of burly men proceeded to liberate the former.

One grasped the saucepan, and the other Tom's legs, and by dint of a vigorous effort, the culinary utensil was at last forcibly dragged from its remarkably strong hold, and Tom's head was once more at liberty.

The idea of being able to eat once more was too much for him to contemplate all at once, and, after sneezing twice, and informing the bystanders "that he wasn't done for yet," fell on his back, and was carried off to bed, instead of leading his gallant, but scattered troop, to the *Koorisades.*

CHAPTER XI.

A MONTH AFTER THE EARL'S DEPARTURE—LADY GODIVA'S NIGHT RAMBLE IN THE GARDEN—LORD OTHNIEL SURPRISES HER IN HER MEDITATIONS—HIS FIRST STEP, AND THE RESULT.

A MONTH had passed since the noble Leofric, Earl of Mercia, had started on his long and perilous journey.

The bearing of Othniel towards the beautiful wife of his friend had been, despite the fierce and turbulent desires that smouldered in his breast, ready to burst forth upon the first opportunity, marked with knightly courtesy and respect, though a close observer might have noticed the lurid fire of his dark eye and the ardent, impassioned glances he cast upon the fair countess whenever he approached her.

It was with the utmost difficulty he restrained the fierce passions that inwardly consumed him within due bounds.

It was no merit on his part that he did so, but he was awed by the chaste and modest demeanour of the woman whom he regarded with such passionate though concealed emotion.

Lawless, unscrupulous, remorseless as was Othniel Raven, still there was something in the tender, respectful devotion with which the Lady Godiva spoke of her absent husband that checked his guilty aspirations, and compelled him in his inmost soul to feel abashed before the simple power of virtue's holy image.

The countess herself, whose constant heart garnered up the memory of her absent lord, was unceasing in her prayers for his safety and speedy return, little deeming the fatal passion she had aroused in the breast of him in whose power—did he choose to exercise it—she might almost be said to be.

As, however, the secrets of the human heart are known only to its owner and its Creator, so the Lady Godiva was for the present utterly unconscious of the peril by which she was surrounded.

It was a lovely night; the moon cast her soft light upon the massive buttresses and battlements of the castle, bringing out every separate wing as definitely as in the broad daylight, and cast fantastic shadows across the garden walks, that quivered and danced as the soft evening breeze stirred the luxuriant shrubs and the branches of the trees, to which they owed their brief existence.

The Lady Godiva was frequently in the habit of walking in the garden at the silent hour when the world was hushed in sleep, and on this night, tempted by the calm quiet of the scene, descended thither, and wended, with dreamy eyes and abstracted thoughts, through the embowered paths, fragrant with roses and sweet briar, whose exquisite perfume the night dew appeared to absorb, whilst the breeze wafted it around.

She wandered on almost unconsciously till she came to a lovely arbour, completely embedded in a mass of foliage.

This beautiful and tranquil spot was a favourite resort of her husband, and here they had often sat together in the summer evenings, recalling the past, and planning undertakings for the future.

Now that husband, that beloved partner of her joys and sorrows, was no longer by her side, and the place seemed silent and deserted.

The quiet beauty of the night seemed to add to the solitude, and never since the departure of the earl, had she seemed so much alone as at that moment.

"Oh, Leofric, husband of my heart," she exclaimed, as she raised her tear-dimmed eyes to the pale luminary, whose unchanging lustre seemed almost to mock her sadness, "where art art thou this moment? Does sleep close thine eyes, or art thou thinking of thy wife as she thinks of thee? Heaven bless and preserve thee, dear one, where'er thou art, and bring thee back to me in safety."

She had clasped her hands involuntarily, and sank upon her knees as she uttered these words, and remained in that position like some beautiful statue, and looking, in the moonlight, as pale and marble-like.

A slight motion on the gravel-walk attracted her attention, and a shadow passed as from behind her; she turned, and, to her surprise, beheld Lord Othniel standing at a short distance from where she knelt, with his arms folded across his breast, gazing upon her with looks of undisguised admiration.

"My Lord Othniel!" she exclaimed, rising from her knees, "you here? I thought I was alone."

"I trust you do not consider my presence an intrusion, fair Godiva?" he said.

"The presence of a friend is never such," she answered. "But when we believe ourselves entirely unwatched, save by that one all-seeing eye that never sleeps, we are apt to unloose our tongues, and pour out our hearts in words we should scarcely use even in the presence of the dearest friend."

"True," replied Othniel; "though having been an involuntary listener to your supplication, I confess I could detect no single word that needs to be regretted, or that fails to attest the piety and faith of the speaker. Happy! thrice happy is my friend Leofric in the possession of a wife, whose beauty is equalled by her virtues!"

"I shall chide you, my lord," she said, "if you flatter me."

"By heavens!" replied Othniel, warmly. "I flatter not. How can words be flattery, when prompted by beauty like yours? Be not offended if I speak earnestly; or, if you are, I must e'en risk your displeasure, for my emotions cannot be controlled."

"My lord!" exclaimed the countess, surprised at the warm enthusiasm of Lord Othniel's speech, and the vivid flush upon his dark countenance, even in that pale light.

"I would say," continued Othniel, eagerly, "that I yearn as eagerly as the slave pants for freedom, to enjoy your friendship"——

"Do you not enjoy it?" interrupted the countess, rather hastily.

"Yes, I hope so, I trust so," he replied; "but I do not mean the ordinary cold acquaintanceship that in the world passes for the name. That may satisfy some temperaments, but not mine. I crave a deeper sentiment—a full confidence a-union"——

"My lord," again interrupted the countess hastily, as if to put an end to words that appeared to be growing warmer than her character would allow her to listen to unrebuked, "be assured that all the friendship I have to bestow, consistent with my own and my husband's honour, will be freely given to that husband's friend.

And now, my lord, it grows late. You will pardon me if I return to the castle."

The countess spoke with a dignity, against which there was no appeal.

She detected in the voice and manner of her husband's friend something which, if it did not alarm her delicacy, at least produced an impression that was unpleasant, and excited a feeling almost akin to suspicion.

Othniel was not slow to divine her thoughts, and endeavoured to remove it.

"Allow me to conduct you to the gate, madam," he said, respectfully tendering his arm as he spoke, "and if I have inadvertently, in word or act, offended where I most earnestly desire to please, attribute it to the weakness of poor mortal nature that, basking in the rays of more than earthly beauty, becomes dazzled and bewildered in its intoxicating splendour."

He offered his arm with the greatest respect as he spoke.

The countess, having no particular excuse for rejecting this courtesy, placed her arm lightly within his, but the touch, light as it was, thrilled through his veins like liquid fire.

They were silent, and continued so until they reached the gate.

It was a silence that had in it something of embarrassment.

Othniel knew perfectly well his own intentions. He felt also that his first attempt to sound, as it were, the feelings of the countess, previous to an attempt to undermine the strong citadel of her affections, had been detected, and failed.

Not by any means susceptible to shame, still Othniel felt humiliated and vexed with himself that he had been too precipitate.

"I trust we part friends, fair Godiva?" he said, as they reached the gate.

"Friends, undoubtedly," replied the amiable countess, who began already to think she might possibly have been misjudging her husband's friend; "and such I trust we ever shall be. And if I have seemed, from my words, to imply a shadow of suspicion, a wife who loves her husband needs scarcely an apology for her endeavour to guard his honour from the slightest breath that would sully or tarnish it."

He bowed, and taking her white hand respectfully in his own, pressed it lightly to his lips.

"Good night, lady," he exclaimed, "this lovely evening will woo me for another hour. I shall remain here, and pray that none but happy dreams may hover round your pillow."

"Where the thoughts are pure, dreams, which are but their echoes, will be pure also, and purity is happiness. Good night, my lord."

No sooner had the countess disappeared, than Othniel placed a small whistle to his mouth and blew it twice.

This was answered by the presence of a man of most unpromising aspect, who advanced from a shrubbery near at hand.

"Wolfhart!" exclaimed Othniel.

"The same, my lord," answered the man.

"'Tis well," returned his lordship; "let us walk this way."

He listened for a moment at the portal, and then, beckoning the man to follow, they proceeded to a more retired part of the garden.

CHAPTER XII.

LADY GODIVA SEES THE STRANGE MAN FROM THE WINDOW — SHE LISTENS AND OVERHEARS A TERRIBLE PLOT—SHE IS SEIZED BY OTHNIEL, AND RESCUED BY THE SPIRIT OF ST. OSBURG—SUDDEN APPEARANCE OF THE SKELETON MONK.

THE Lady Godiva on entering the castle proceeded at once to her sleeping apartment.

Guileless and pure in her own imaginings, unsuspicious as a child of dangers she had never yet had to encounter, she was nevertheless shaken in her opinion of Lord Raven on this night.

On entering her chamber she looked out once more upon the quiet and lovely night. To her surprise she beheld Lord Othniel speaking to one who was to her an entire stranger.

She noticed the air of caution with which he looked around, and the furtive reconnoitring glance he threw up towards the window of her apartment; and, in spite of herself, she felt an uncontrollable inward presentiment that some evil was contemplated, either against her or someone as dear to her as her own life. She tried to banish these thoughts from her mind; but as Othniel and his myrmidon disappeared in the shadows of the shrubbery, they rushed into her mind with redoubled force. She was averse to anything approaching meanness or mistrust, and yet she was prompted by some hidden impulse with an intense desire to listen to the conversation of Lord Raven and his mysterious companion.

This desire grew stronger and stronger, till she could no longer restrain it.

Her mind was soon decided.

She resolved to descend once more into the garden, and, by making a short circuit, to reach, unseen and unsuspected, the spot where Othniel and his companion were located.

She abhorred, as every generous mind does, the contemptible habit of eavesdropping, but she felt that in this case the end justified the means.

Actuated by this feeling she descended the stairs and cautiously took her way towards the extremity of the garden.

It was not long before she heard the voices of his lordship and the stranger, who were standing at a short distance from the arbour she had so lately quitted.

With a step light as the antelope's, and scarcely daring to breathe, lest the sound should betray her presence, she cautiously drew near the spot where the conference was carrying on.

The moon fell full upon the countenance of Wolfhart.

Whatever this individual might have been in his moral character, his external physical appearance was far from prepossessing.

An inflammatory, blotchy-looking complexion; a broad, low forehead, surmounted by a mass of coarse, black hair, that time was beginning to sprinkle with grey; a harsh, wiry beard, that looked as though no ordinary comb in its senses would have dared to attempt the task of disentangling; and the whole of these personal peculiarities, heightened by the addition of a large and deep scar across his brow, completed a picture which, in its general effect, was ogreish and revolting.

Such was Wolfhart in appearance—a man who, however unpromising in external signs, had one good quality—fidelity to his employer.

He was what, in modern theatrical language, might have been termed a sort of general utility man to Lord Othniel.

He had been for some time his servant, tool, agent, or whatever people liked to call him, he himself having no choice at all in the matter.

Whatever scheme his master's evil brain devised, his was the strong arm and the dogged, unflinching spirit to execute; and he had now been summoned from Othniel's castle in Yorkshire on a mission of importance.

As the Lady Godiva reached the spot where master and slave were standing, the conference had just commenced.

"Wolfhart," said Lord Othniel, "you know that on many past occasions I have honoured you with special confidence. Whenever I have had any enterprise of particular importance or difficulty to undertake I have invariable entrusted it to you."

"Your lordship is perfectly right," answered Wolfhart. "This scar on my forehead, this hand minus a finger"—indicating the embellishments alluded to as he spoke—"and six dagger wounds in different parts of my body, are proofs of the difficulties of your enterprises, and of my courage and determination in carrying them out."

"I am not dissatisfied with your services," remarked Lord Raven; "and I am now about to entrust you with a commission far more important than all the rest."

"What is it, your lordship?" inquired Wolfhart.

"I am going to send you to Palestine," returned Othniel.

"Oh!" briefly remarked Wolfhart, without betraying the least surprise or emotion, but acting as though a journey to the Holy Land—every morning before breakfast, had it been possible — would have been quite a simple and common-place occurrence.

Godiva, in her place of ambush, at the mention of the Holy Land, found her interest immediately excited.

"You do not appear surprised at this," remarked Lord Raven.

"I'm never surprised at anything, your lordship," was the cool reply.

"Then you are willing to undertake this journey?"

"Undoubtedly : that is," he continued, "if I'm well paid for it."

"You shall be handsomely rewarded, depend upon it," answered Othniel.

"And how am I to reach Palestine? and what am I to do when I get there?" inquired Wolfhart.

"I am about to inform you," returned his master. "The Count Hubert de Bracy is about to lead a force to the Holy Land. You will join his troop under the protest that you are tired of an idle life at home, and wish for foreign service."

"And when I arrive, what then?"

"You know Earl Leofric of Mercia?" he inquired, leaning forward and fixing his stern eyes scrutinizingly upon the man he was addressing.

"By sight, well," answered Wolfhart; "a noble kind of giant—I know him."

"I loved his wife in years gone by, but she preferred him to me, and so I lost her."

"Umph ! that was awkward."

"It was maddening at the time; however. as you see," he added, with a grim smile, "I contrived to get over it, though I still love her. The earl's departure to the holy wars leaves the field of beauty open to me, and I now intend, after patiently waiting some years, that she shall be mine."

"There's only one obstacle that seems to me to stand in the way, and that is *your* being married and *she* being married," remarked Wolfhart.

"Psha ! these obstacles must be removed, do you understand me?" he inquired, in a searching tone.

"Perfectly," said Wolfhart, bluntly; "you want him dead, and I'm to kill him."

"Yes," exclaimed Othniel; "you must contrive to get near him in the heat of battle and strike him with your dagger; and to make sure the blow is effectual, and, to put his fate beyond a doubt, see that the steel be poisoned ; and "——

At this juncture a faint cry of anguish was heard.

Both started.

The voice seemed familiar.

Whence did it proceed?

They searched in the immediate vicinity, and in a few moments discovered the countess, prostrate and senseless on the ground.

The horrible truth she had heard had crushed her down like an electric shock, and she lay bereft of sense or motion.

"Curses on this mischance !" muttered Othniel. "Can she have heard?"

"No doubt of it," said Wolfhart, consolingly ; "and if she is in possession of the secret, it strikes me we shall have to cut *her* throat as well, or she'll blab."

"Silence, scoundrel !" exclaimed Lord Raven, angrily ; "you'll be content with cutting such throats as I appoint, and none other."

"Certainly, my lord." answered the man. submissively. "But with respect to this little business over in Palestine, how much am I to have for executing it?"

"Two hundred marks shall be your reward," replied his lordship.

"I'll do it," cried the ruffian, his sinister countenance brightening up into some such ferocious gleam of good humour as would have delighted a tiger cat; "I'll do it—but as this is a world of chances in which there's many a slip between the cup and the lip, I think half the money down will be a very fair arrangement."

Othniel looked earnestly into the eyes of his unscrupulous agent, and after a moment's pause assented to this arrangement.

"Come with me," he cried. "I will place the money in your hands at once."

They were about to leave the spot when, to their great surprise, they found themselves confronted by the Lady Godiva herself.

At the first shock of the terrible mission she had heard terrified humanity had recoiled and she had fainted; but the atrocious plot formed against one so dear to her as her husband speedily aroused her from her short lethargy, and inspired her with the indignant fury of a Nemesis.

"Oh, noble lord! oh, generous friend! oh, honourable knight!" she cried; "that can thus conspire against a brother in arms! Shame on you! you disgrace the title you bear. But I will proclaim you in every corner of the city; the youngest child that passes you shall know you as a traitor and a perjurer!"

Having uttered these words she rushed from the spot; but her pursuers were fleet of foot, and, ere she could reach the door of the castle, her flight was arrested.

"Not so fast, my gentle fury," cried Lord Othniel, attempting to embrace her.

This was a somewhat dangerous experiment to try, for it placed her in dangerous proximity with the dagger that was suspended to his lordship's girdle.

In an instant she had grasped the handle and drawn it from the sheath, and in the next, with almost savage desperation, she presented the keen point to the throat of Lord Raven.

"Recal the fatal mandate you have given this wretch!" she cried, so fiercely that no one would have recognised the usually gentle tones of her voice in the stern accents that fell from her quivering lips; "recal it, I say, while you have yet the power!"

A mocking laugh from the *wretch* was the only answer, and in an instant the dagger was forcibly wrenched from her hand, whilst the strong arm of Othniel encircled her.

"Harkye, lady," he hissed in her ear; "it was my intention to show you every courtesy—to woo and win you fairly if possible, but you yourself have frustrated my intentions. You know my secret, and, in self-defence, I must now coerce your actions, fetter your limbs, and woo you in the dark. The vaults beneath the castle will tell no tales, and thither will I convey you. Come!"

It was in vain the unhappy woman pleaded for her liberty; her assailant was deaf to her entreaties.

She trembled as she looked upon that swarthy countenance and those fierce, passionate eyes, and felt as though heaven itself had forsaken her.

A deadly sensation of overpowering faintness passed over her frame. She recollected hear-ing the distant bell toll forth the hour of midnight, and that, at the last stroke of the bell, a wild strain of music, unearthly in its sweetness, floated all around them.

A deep awe fell upon the soul of the guilty Othniel, and not less upon the equally unscrupulous but more ignorant Wolfhart, as, before them in the path, stood a bright and beautiful figure, surrounded by a dazzling halo of more than mortal lustre.

Lord Raven released his helpless victim as though impelled by some unseen but resistless power, whilst she staggered forward, conscious of her innocence, and fell upon her knees before the beautiful apparition.

"Oh, save me, sainted spirit! Save me!" she cried earnestly.

"Fear not!" answered the glorious being, in a voice whose every tone was melody; "your foes are powerless to harm you; the spirit of St. Osburg watches over you. Man of unholy thoughts!" she cried sternly to Othniel, who glared at her with blanched cheeks, and trembling limbs. "*Beware!*"

The spirit raised her arms in an attitude of benediction over Godiva's head, and gradually both appeared to glide away, till they were no longer visible.

Othniel, when he no longer saw the form that had appalled his conscience-stricken spirit, recovered his usual recklessness.

Drawing his sword, he shouted to Wolfhart, who was crouched down on the ground making frantic efforts — but in vain—to remember a single prayer.

"Follow me!"

The terrified ruffian obeyed, when, as they reached the castle porch, a tall figure, enveloped in a grey cloak and hood slowly stepped forth.

"Beware!" it cried, in a freezing tone.

The cowl fell back, and disclosed the ghastly lineaments of—*the Skeleton Monk!*

With a loud cry of horror Othniel Raven staggered back and sank prostrate on the ground, whilst the terrified myrmidon, of his guilt rushed with headlong speed from the spot.

CHAPTER XIII.

PEEPING TOM, AFTER KEEPING HIS ROOM FOR SOME TIME, BECOMES CONVALESCENT — HE RESOLVES TO PAY ANOTHER VISIT TO THE CASTLE GARDEN WITH HIS FRIENDS — HE CLIMBS A TREE, AND COMES DOWN AGAIN RATHER SUDDENLY, WHERE HE MEETS WITH AN ADVENTURE.

MORE than a month had passed away since Peeping Tom, in his desire to distinguish himself as a warrior of renown, had very nearly extinguished himself in his granny's garden.

His band of heroes had been ignominiously put to flight by the formidable crutched stick of Dame Winker, and General Tom once more reduced to a state of vassalage, penitence and fasting, the worthy old dame being resolved to bring him to a sense of his iniquities by a wholesome austerity in his diet.

Thick slices of bread without butter and total abstinence from the delights of gingerbread and ale had brought the delinquent Tom to a state of humility and obedience that was highly delightful to the old lady, who informed her gossipping friend, Mrs. Trumper, that Tom was entirely changed ; that he had undergone a perfect moral renovation ; and was henceforth going to be an ornament to society, and a model to grandsons in general.

To a certain extent this was true, while Tom was smarting under the stripes of his grandmother's sturdy blackthorn, whilst his excoriated nose throbbed and swelled, and looked like two or three noses that had gone into partnership, and whilst, added to these sensations, he writhed under an incipient bilious attack, which his worthy relative was endeavouring to dislodge by her universal panacea of salts and senna, he lay moaning and groaning, and heaping upon himself in addition to the bed-clothes, all kinds of self-reproaches.

"Don't yer feel yer've been a very wicked boy?" his old granny would say shaking her head in a most anathematical manner, as she contemplated him through her spectacles with somewhat severe eyes, and at the same time stirred up some nauseous compound with a spoon for his especial benefit. "Don't yer feel yer deserves your sufferins, eh? Don't yer deserve to die, an' be put underground, eh? eh?"

"Oh yes, I does, I does! I knows I'm a going to die this time!" whined Tom in a doleful voice.

Upon which his granny, having worked him up to a proper state of terror, artfully introduced the senna draught as the only possible means of saving him at such a perilous crisis.

By these means Tom was induced to swallow a considerable quantity of this unsavoury beverage — 'buckets full'—so he declared when he became convalescent, and to lie in bed counting the patches in the quilt, and contemplating his toes, which he thrust out at the side, his legs not being long enough to permit him to perform that feat from the bottom.

However, as the days passed, the stripes became less painful, the bilious qualms, and gripings subsided, and the excoriated nose began to heal, and quietly drop into its usual state, and, as a natural consequence, Tom began to grumble—the ungrateful sinner—at the bed with the patchwork quilt, and dry bread without any butter, and to sigh once more for society, ale, and gingerbread.

There was nothing of these luxuries at his granny's cottage.

His rational enjoyments were limited to pelting the dog Tinker, as he lay in his kennel, ducking the cat, which operation he usually performed two or three times a day, and stirring up the pig with the garden rake.

But even these amusements, exciting and delightful as they undoubtedly were for a time, still, when persisted in day after day, they became tinged with a monotony that ceased to charm.

Had gunpowder happened to have been invented, what blissful joys would have been his!

Then he could have tied crackers to Tinker's tail, and blown up the cottage, and his granny into the bargain, to say nothing of blowing off two or three of his own fingers.

But as gunpowder was not (fortunately for Tom's immediate neighbours) invented, no such stirring enjoyments could be procured, and he began to puzzle his brains what to be after.

Suddenly his thoughts reverted to the garden of the castle, with its gooseberries and peaches.

Certainly there were some passing shadows flitting across the prospect in the shape of the irate gardener and the hungry bloodhound, but they were merely incidents in the drama—trifling sensations that added to the general effect and enjoyment of the undertaking.

"The goosegogs'll be over," said Tom, to himself ; "but the currants'll be in, an' the plums an' greengages—an' don't I like them? Oh!" he accompanied this self-put question by a most cordial and affirmative rubbing of his stomach, and a smacking of the lips that would have startled Dame Winker had she heard it.

His mind was made up.

He would visit the castle garden once more.

Accordingly, on the very next afternoon, whilst his granny was taking her afternoon nap, he quietly stole forth.

Tom, thinking that his friends might be glad to find that he still survived the perils and sufferings he had undergone, made a complete round of calls ; the consequence of which was, that, by the time he reached the castle walls, he had devoured a bar of gingerbread and drank several pints of ale, which, he observed to Dick, who, with several more of his friends, had accompanied him, "put new life into him, and made him feel another creetur altogether."

After a little consultation as to who should mount the wall first, the choice, as usual, fell upon Tom, who was invariably the scapegoat in all these expeditions.

Accordingly, Tom was hoisted up by the boys, and reached the top with a succession of "Oh—oh's!" and "Oh, dont's!" where he sat astride and pulled two or three pins out of the calves of his legs, with which his facetious pals beneath had accommodated him.

"Oh, you shouldn't!" he cried, rubbing the offended members ; "pins is sharp remember. Besides, yer might ha' stuck one in a wein, an' then there'd ha' been a pretty go! I should ha' bled to death."

"Never mind your calves, Tom," cried Dick ; "think of the plums. Any one about?"

Tom did think of the plums, and looked down with all his eyes into the garden, but no living soul could be seen ; neither was anything heard but the twittering of the birds.

Everything looked beautifully quiet and tempting.

"It's all right," said Tom, who sat astride the wall in a state of exulting rapture. "Come on," he cried to those beneath ; "the plums do look prime. There's sich a bloom on 'em!" in his delirious joy he jumped himself up and down on the wall as though he might have been riding an imaginary trotting race, and presently sat on a sharp nail that was sticking bolt upright all ready for his express accommodation.

"Oh! oh! oh!" he yelled, starting up, and rubbing himself vigorously. "Pins in the calves is bad enough, but nails where yer sits down is awful."

"Give us a hand up," cried Dick, from beneath.

Tom forgot the anguish of the nail in a moment ; and, leaning down along the top of the wall, assisted his companion to mour

One after the other they ascended, and perched themselves on the summit like a flock of mischievous sparrows.

"Come on," said Tom. "It's no good our a sittin' 'ere all day, an' leavin' the fruit for the birds. Come on—down we go."

"All right," cried mischievous Dick, giving Tom a sudden leg-up, which overbalanced him, and dropped him on his back in the mould in the garden.

"Oh crikey!" said Tom. "That was rather too quick."

He was speedily hoisted on to his feet, and rubbed down, and patted and punched by his friends, till he declared, "he was all right."

"Where shall we begin?" asked Harry. "You've been here before, and know the way about."

"We'll begin with the currants fust, the black uns', I'm fond o' black currants."

Accordingly, they proceeded to the currant bushes, and commenced operations with great spirit.

"Ain't it prime?" cried Tom, picking and eating as if for a wager.

"How many slugs have you swallowed, Tom?" cried Dick.

"Only four or five," he answered; "but I don't mind them, 'cos as they live's upon currants, they tastes 'xactly the same as currants."

The boys laughed.

"I've had enough o' these," remarked Tom, after he had eaten two or three quarts; "let's be off to the plum trees."

This proposal being agreed to, they proceeded down a narrow alley that led to a kind of orchard, in which were a quantity of the above trees.

Tom was instantly hoisted up into one of them, with strict injunctions to pick as many as he could, and throw them down to his friends beneath.

Tom, however, who had a particular weakness for this fruit, finding himself in such close proximity to the plums, picked away to his heart's content, and gobbled as fast as he picked.

This did not, however, suit his colleagues below.

"Tom," cried Dick, "you're a glutton. You're eating all the plums yourself!"

"Oh, what a story! I'm sure I ain't," said Tom, stuffing three into his mouth at once, and becoming slightly convulsed up at the top of the tree, in his efforts to bolt them.

"Oh, lor'!" he exclaimed to himself, "I thought I never should ha' got rid o' that lot. What a awful thing it must be to be choked!"

"Now, then, slow coach!" called Dick, "how much longer are we to wait for the plums?"

"I'm a pickin' 'em as fast as ever I can," answered Tom, looking up at a remarkably fine fat plum, some little distance over his head, and resolving to secure it, or perish in the attempt."

"You mean you're eating them," cried the boys.

Tom at this moment made a sudden stretch forward, and clutched the coveted plum, and in so doing very nearly pitched headlong to the ground.

"Now I've got yer," he murmured, popping it into his mouth.

It is a delicious plum; but his sensations of perfect enjoyment were disturbed by a shower of stones from his impatient companions below.

"Oh, oh," cried Tom," as the stones rattled about him. "Come, stash it."

"Throw down some plums, then," cried the boys.

"I'm a-going to," he answered. "I must give 'em some," he soliloquized, "or they'll be a-shyin' brickbats or flower-pots at me, or somethink o' that sort."

Possessed with this idea, he hit upon the expedient of supplying them in a wholesale manner.

He climbed up higher into the tree, and, clasping the trunk, began to shake it with all his might.

The effect was immense.

Down came the plums as thick as hail.

The boys were delighted, and, unable to control their emotion, shouted for joy.

"Ain't that somethink like plums?" cried Tom. enthusiastically.

"Bravo, Tom!" they answered, with one voice.

"Go it again, old fellow!" shouted Dick. "We'll take home enough to make some jam."

"Jam!" echoed Tom. smacking his lips. "Won't that be plummy?"

Thus expressing himself, he continued the shaking, and the plums continued dropping till the foragers were tolerably well loaded.

"'Ere goes for a last one," he cried.

He grasped the branch, and was about to administer a more severe oscillation than ever, when the ominous baying of the terrible bloodhound was heard at a very short distance from the spot.

"Oh, lor'!" cried Tom, in a terrified voice; "it's that there dawg."

The boys looked at one another.

"I say, Harry," said Dick, "do you like dogs?"

"Not particularly," answered Harry; "especially when they drop on to us in other people's gardens."

"It's my opinion," remarked Joe, "the sooner we're on the other side of the wall, the better."

"Bow, wow, wow!—woo, woo, woo!" barked the hound, with great gusto.

"He barks as if he meant it," cried Dick. "Come along, boys!"

"But what's to become of fat old Tom up there?" inquired Bill.

"Oh, he'll be all right!" said Dick. "He always manages to come off square; besides, he's so precious fat; the dog can't get at him anywhere."

"Bow, wow, wow!" again howled the dog.

"Come on," cried Dick. "Come on, Tom; here's the dog loose."

Away scampered the troop, leaving Tom in an indescribable state of horror at the top of the plum tree.

"Oh, lor'! Oh, dear!" he cried. "What hever shall I do? If that 'ere bloodthirsty dawg catches sight o' me he'll eat me alive."

"Woo, woo, woo!" answered the dog, affirmatively.

"Oh, don't I wish as I was safe in bed, under the patchwork quilt! Oh, ain't I been a bad boy to granny!" groaned the unhappy Tom. "I shall never live to eat these plums when they're made into jam," he added, alluding to a pocket full he had collected with that intention; "so I may as well eat 'em now."

"Dick ! Harry !" he shouted, as well as he could, considering his mouth was full.

But no answer came.

Dick, Harry, Joe, and Bill were safely perched on a wall at a part that was concealed by shrubs, but which allowed them to see what was going on below in the garden.

Being out of danger themselves, the unfeeling young ruffians were waiting anxiously to enjoy the fun of seeing Tom engaged in single combat with the bloodhound.

Tom in the meantime receiving no answer, became possessed of horrors indescribable.

"Dick ! Tom ! Joe !" he roared, between every plum. "Oh, do come, that's good fellows."

The conviction at last forced himself upon him that they had taken to their heels and left him to shift for himself.

"Oh, whatever shall I do?" he groaned, "the hidear o' their a' goin' an' leavin' me stuck up 'ere in the top of a plum tree to be devoured by that 'ungry blood'ound."

"Bow, wow, wow !" barked the brute.

"Oh lor' !" cried Tom, "I'll get right up to the tip top an' then he wont see me. But then, wot's the good o' that ? If he can't see me he'll smell me, so I'm sure to be cotched, any'ow."

However, carrying out his intention of climbing higher in the tree, he forgot that he was heavy and that the higher he mounted the thinner the branches became.

A violent "bow, wow, wow," infused a desperate earnestness into his efforts to perch himself on the topmost bough, where he might be invisible, and where the breeze might waft away any *Tom Winker*-ish odours that might cling to him and remind the bloodhound of his proximity.

In a state of intense trepidation he made a violent grab at a branch a story higher. He grasped the desired support, but, alas! it was not strong enough to bear Tom with his cargo of currants and plums ; and the consequence was that our hero came crashing through the branches headlong to the ground, just as the hungry bloodhound, with his bloodshot eyes and bloodthirsty-looking open jaws, came tearing up to the spot to see whether some benevolent fairy, who had a partiality for the canine species, had dropped some luxury in the shape of a paunch or a pluck from the plum tree. Tom curled himself up like a corpulent hedgehog without his bristles. He wished he had had some bristles; in fact, he would have given the world if he could have been at once converted into a porcupine.

The bloodhound in the meantime, walked round growling and opening his wide jaws, apparently puzzled to know whether Tom was fish, flesh, or fowl ; whilst Tom, in a state of horrible apprehension, was endeavouring to resign himself as patiently as possible to the unpleasant fate of being eaten alive.

CHAPTER XIV.

Tom excites the dwarf's curiosity, who stirs him up with his dagger—Tom and the bloodhound go to war in the garden—a critical situation—and how Peeping Tom got out of it.

No sooner had Earl Leofric departed for the crusades, than Othniel, under some pretence or other, dismissed all the old servants, whose places he refilled by creatures of his own.

This was naturally enough a cause of sorrow to the kind-hearted Lady Godiva, who would fain have appealed in their behalf, but the reasons given by Othniel for their dismissal were so plausible, that she, to her sorrow, was compelled to desist from her ineffectual entreaties. The only two of the earl's domestics retained were Delve, the gardener, and a pretty little dark-eyed damsel named Una, who waited on the countess.

Una Brandon was a native of Coventry, or rather a few miles out of the town, where her fath₅ cultivated a small farm.

She was a good-natured, kind-hearted little body, whose rosy charms had on one occasion made an impression on the sensitive heart of Tom Winker ; but when she went into the earls' service he did not meet her as often as when she lived in the capacity of waitress at the "Conqueror" Inn in the market, and other things, especially ale and gingerbread, coming in the way to distract him, he had entirely forgotten there was such a person in the world.

Little, too, did she deem that her corpulent hobbedyhoy *quondam* sweetheart was at that moment in such imminent peril.

This, however, did not at all alter the fact that he was so.

The bloodhound walked round and round with his fiery eyes and his gaping jaws, lashing his tail and longing to commence operations upon Tom, but not knowing where to begin.

A new arrival, however, upon the scene soon relieved him from this anxiety.

This was no other than Lord Raven's dwarf, Ghoul.

In size he was very diminutive, not being more than three feet high. From his appearance he had evidently arrived at man's estate, and his features were a compound of cunning, sarcasm, mischief, and cruelty.

His head was unnaturally large for his size, and ornamented with a pair of ears of most unsightly appearance.

His forehead protruded and his eyes receded, the latter members being small and piggish, and flashing with green and red lights.

His cheeks were drawn in and withered to the colour of old parchment, whilst a set of discoloured fangs, that were supposed to be teeth, protruded from a wide, terrible mouth.

Some dry elf locks, of a dusty brown, straggled scantily upon his head, and a small tuft of the same non-luxuriant material grew on his chin.

He appeared to be all body and head ; his legs being short and like two spindles, whilst his arms were preternaturally long and indicative of more strength than the lower members of his corporeal frame.

He was not exactly hump-backed, but a roundness in the shoulders gave him somewhat the appearance of possessing this deformity.

His attire was somewhat fantastic, and in the colour and fashion of his garb, which was a mixture of scarlet and black, he appeared to have consulted his own fancy rather than the fashion of the period ; one peculiarity was a comical hat, very diproportionate to the size of his enormous head which he contrived to

LADY GODIVA;

OR, PEEPING TOM OF COVENTRY.

THE LADY OF COVENTRY.

keep perched in its place on a tuft of bristly hair that stuck upon the centre of his skull.

A small, curved scimitar of foreign appearance, double-edged towards the point, hung at his waist, and though not much larger than a dagger that a man might have worn, was much too formidable to be regarded as a child's toy.

His walk was a kind of waddle, consequent upon the shortness of his legs; and, having noticed the savage haste with which the bloodhound had rushed into the orchard, he followed as fast as he was able to ascertain the cause of the animal's excitement.

Great was the surprise of Ghoul when he reached the spot where Tom, quaking with terror, lay coiled up under the plum tree.

"Ho, ho!" said he; "what strange fish is this? What is it, Lion?" he repeated, appealing to the dog, and peering curiously down upon Tom out of his little, keen pig eyes.

Lion whined and lashed his tail, and snapped his formidable jaws, from which the saliva dripped as though in eager anticipation of a coming banquet.

"Ho, ho!" sung out Ghoul; "I can see that delicate mouth of yours waters, Lion. You're hungry ain't you, old boy?"

"Wow! wow! wow!" barked Lion, affirmatively.

"Oh lor! oh dear!" groaned Tom, who had been aroused by the harsh, croaking voice of the dwarf, and slily taken a peep at him through his fingers; "what a horrid, bloodthirsty-looking little wretch."

The little wretch in question had grown tired of examining Tom as a curiosity, and was becoming desirous to know all about him.

He approached; and, placing his arms akimbo, and assuming a magisterial sternness of manner and an authoritative tone of voice, commanded—

"Are you alive or dead?"

"I'm alive, I think," answered Tom with some hesitation, as though he was not quite sure of the fact.

"Who are you?" continued the dwarf, sternly.

"I—I'm Tom Winker."

"Oh, you're Tom Winker, are you. And who, in the name of Diabolus and all the other Bolusses, is Tom Winker?"

"I told you," said Tom; "it's me."

"I don't know any such caitiff as Tom Winker," replied the dwarf, grandly.

"I'm called Peeping Tom of Coventry," continued Tom, in an explanatory manner, as though that title would have been sufficient to settle everything.

"Ah!" exclaimed the dwarf, reflectively; "I have heard of a base muck-worm of that name."

"I ain't a muck-worm," humbly suggested Tom.

"Silence!" cried Ghoul; "slaves are not allowed to make remarks. This peeping caitiff, so I heard once, dared to intrude his vile body over yonder garden wall."

"Oh lor'!" groaned Tom.

"And what d'ye think he did?"

"I don't know," faltered the peeping caitiff.

"He devoured six quarts of gooseberries, three dozen peaches; demolished a melon frame and pulled down a grape vine, besides kicking the poor dog in the jaw. Lion!" he shouted, with sudden and violent emphasis; "he kicked you on the jaw, good dog; don't forget it."

"Wow! wow! wow!" barked the hound, which, literally translated, meant "I won't."

Tom's heart sank within him.

The dwarf, with the utmost deliberation, drew his scimitar; and, with dreadful coolness, passed his thumb along both sides of the edge, and made believe to stab himself in the palm of his hand.

"He's a tryin' if it's sharp enough," murmured Tom who happened to take a peep at that moment. "Oh dear! it's all over with me."

"Now, what do you think," continued the dwarf, "such an unlimited gorging, rapacious glutton deserves, eh? eh?"

Tom was suddenly seized with a weakness in his intellect, and couldn't imagine.

"I'll tell you what he deserves!" sternly went on Ghoul. "First, he ought to be pricked all over with this," as he spoke giving poor Tom a prog with the awful scimitar, that made every drop of blood in his body run cold, "that would let out the juice of the gooseberries"——

"Oh!" cried Tom.

"Then I should like, mounted on Lion's back, to hunt him round the garden; after which, I would recline on a seat whilst the dog worried him, and finally I should rip up the vile churl with my scimitar, and cut off his head. Ho! ho! that's what I should like to do. That's what I should like to do!"

The savage little being had worked himself up to a state of excitement that was perfectly terrible, and danced about, flourishing the terrible scimitar like a fraction of a wild Indian at some bloodthirsty festival.

"And now," he continued, pausing suddenly, "I should like to know what *you* want here?"

"I don't want nothink," whined Tom.

"Don't tell lies!" shouted the dwarf, pricking him with the point of the scimitar.

"I ain't a tellin' lies!" roared Tom. "Oh! oh!" he bellowed, as the point of the scimitar descended twice upon his fat body.

"Sit up!" ordered the dwarf.

Tom obediently sat up, and so did the bloodhound—a most hideous howl, that threw Tom into a paroxysm of terror, and twisted his round face into the likeness of a comic pancake, under temporary difficulties.

"Oh, do keep off the *dorg*, please Mr. Thing-a-my"——

"Ghoul! when you speak to me," corrected the little man.

"Mr. Ghoul, I mean," said Tom submissively.

"When you want *nothing*, do you usually climb up into the top of a plum tree to look for it?" inquired the dwarf, darting a fiery look right into Tom's eye, which made him a *winker* in more senses than one.

"No," answered Tom, thoroughly knocked off his balance by this ferocious pigmy. "I climb up a plum tree when I want plums."

This was undoubtedly a rash confession, but poor scared Tom hardly knew what he was saying.

"Ha! ha!" shouted the dwarf, flourishing his sword, and repeating the Indian clog dance. "Hear him! shade of *Shiraschalpekill*. Hear him! He confesses the plums! Oho! Oho!"

Tom, who had not the remotest conception who *Shiraschalpekill* might be, looked about wildly, and finally up in the plum tree, fully expecting to see another dwarf, or perhaps a giant, as the owner of the long name.

"So you came here to steal the plums, did you?" said Ghoul, viciously, after rhapsodizing for some time.

"Well, if the truth must be told," answered Tom, who thought perhaps, a candid confession would be the best course to pursue under the circumstances, "I did, but I only had one or two. I gave all the rest to the boys as was with me."

Oh, naughty, untruthful **Tom Winker!**

"Boys! what boys?"

"Dick, Harry, Joe, and Bill—my pals."

"Oh! and where are they?"

"I don't know. All I does know is, as I climbed the tree and chucked the plums down to them, an' when they 'eard the dorg, they bolted, an' left me to get out o' the mess the best way I could."

Ghoul fixed his cunning, penetrating eyes upon Tom, and looked at him for several moments in a most extraordinary manner.

His features twitched and moved convulsively, as though some one had been behind him pulling certain invisible wires.

The sword slashed here and there in appalling closeness to Tom's nose.

The little man kept muttering to himself rather indistinctly certainly, but what Tom did hear was anything but soothing to his feelings. "Ho! ho!" he cried, "oh, I should like—I should like"—slash, slash, with the sword, over and under—"right through him there!"—thrust thrust,—"a slice there!"—slash, slash,—" one of his eyes, the fat swine!"—thrust, thrust—" his right ear!"—a down stroke—"ho! ho!— nose, liver and lights, bowels, ha! ha! ho! ho! ho!"—cut, thrust, slash, up, down, and across, etc., etc.

Having worked himself up to a proper state of frenzy, the dwarf suddenly shouted—

"Lion, good dog."

The hound flew to his side, and, with a jerk, Ghoul mounted on his back.

"Now," cried the dwarf to Tom, with a malignant grin, hooking his toes under the body of the dog, "I'll give yer a minute start. Run like a million hares, because if I catch you I shall kill you. Ho, ho! Run! Fly!"

Tom needed not a second injunction, and set off at full speed.

"I'll be over the wall like a shot," thought Tom, as he pelted down the alley leading into the garden and the gooseberries.

"Dick, 'Arry, Joe, for 'evving's sake, where are yer!" he cried as he ran.

"Here we are, old boy," cried Dick, in his cheeriest, but most treacherous tone.

And there, sure enough, he was, and there were all the rest, comfortably seated in a row, on the top of the wall, out of harm's way.

"Why, where have yer been all this time?" he continued. "Oh, you old rascal, I'll be bound you haven't left a plum on the tree."

"Don't talk about plums, for mussy's sake," cried the agitated Tom. "It's a wonder I ain't been devoured by the dorg."

"Oh, you're all right. No dog would ever eat you; you're too fat," said Dick.

"Oh, but it ain't the dorg so much, it's that 'orrid little dwarf," explained Tom in great anxiety. "Give us a 'and up."

"What dwarf?" asked cold-blooded Dick, coolly, without offering even a finger.

"I'll tell you," cried Tom, in an agony of trepidation, "when I'm on the top of the wall. Oh, do make 'aste! he's on the dorg's back now, a going to 'unt me round the garding."

The boys nudged one another.

Not for worlds would they have lost that hunt.

"Wow, wow, wow," barked the dog.

"'Ere they come!" groaned Tom.

"Give us your hand," said Dick, bending down, but purposely pretending he could not reach him.

"It's no go, Tom," he cried.

"Let yourself down furder," pleaded Tom. "'Arry, 'old on to Dick's legs!"

At this juncture the dwarf's harsh voice was heard.

"Whoo-oop, forward! Lion, good dog! Ho! ho!"

"'Ere they come!" yelled Tom.

"Who?"

"The dwarf an' the dorg."

"Where?"

"There!"

And finding escape by the wall hopeless, away scudded Tom for dear life.

"Whoo-oop! hallo!" rang out through the garden, and out of the alley dashed the blood-hound, with the dwarf on his back, on the track of the persecuted Tom.

Oh, what a thrill of joy passed through the breasts of the boys on the wall!

And, at the same time, what wretched sensations were torturing poor Tom Winker.

"Oh, 'ow I wish I 'adn't ate them plums!" he cried, as he went puffing along; "no one can run after eatin' plums."

The boys shouted vociferously—

"Go it, Tom!"

"Go it, dorg!"

"Go it, Humpty-Dumpty!" which was the title they applied to the dwarf.

The chase was most exciting.

Up one path and down another.

Now, as Humpty-Dumpty and the dorg neared Tom, Tom artfully drops down behind a gooseberry bush, and letting his pursuers gallop past, doubles them and starts off in the opposite direction.

Ghoul soon discovers his mistake, and with a "Ho! ho!" turns round and follows.

The chase cannot continue long.

Ghoul is getting irritated at Tom's dodging powers; the dorg is getting savage with the excitement of the chase; and Tom is labouring under want of breath, and a bellyful of plums and currants.

He pauses for an instant.

He hears the cry of Humpty-Dumpty behind him.

What shall he do to escape?

His eye falls upon a garden rake.

He picks it up with frantic eagerness, and darts behind a frame of scarlet runners.

He is desperate.

He grasps the rake convulsively in his fat hands.

His excitement is intense.

He can feel the plums rolling over and over in his abdominal regions.

He hears his enemies approaching.

Pat, pat, pat, sound the dog's feet.

"Woo! o-o!" he barks short and sharp.

"Forward, good dog!" shrieks the dwarf.

They pass the scarlet-runners.

Swish, goes the rake, and down it falls on the dwarf's head, who rolls over with a crash to the ground, leaving Lion to continue the pursuit alone.

"Take that, yer bloodthirsty little nonde-script!" cried Tom, as he delivered the blow.

"Oh, shade of Inkibobus!" cried the dwarf, as he rolled on the ground, rubbing his head. "Won't I have your liver and lights for this!"

Tom having, as he thought, fractured the dwarf's skull, and so settled matters amicably, made for the wall once more.

This part of the contest had been unseen by the boys, the intervening plants and bushes concealing the view, but Tom heard their voices cheering him on.

"Bravo, Tom ! Bravo everybody ! "

As soon as Tom appeared in sight, rake in hand, they gave him an additional cheer.

"Have you killed 'em both ? " asked Dick.

"No, only one," answered Tom. "I've knocked out that pigmy's brains with this 'ere rake ! "

"And the dog ? " asked Harry.

"I don't know anythin' about him,'" said Tom, " an' I don't want to know. All I want is to get out."

Would it be credited that these hard-hearted youths were not satisfied without witnessing a set-to between Tom and the bloodhound ?

"You should have smashed the *dorg*, Tom, while you were about it," cried the boys.

"He didn't stop to be smashed," answered Tom, " or he would have been smashed, I know —but never mind. I'll come another day and finish him. Give us yer 'and."

The growl of the dog was at this crisis distinctly heard.

"Oh, do help me hup ! " roared Tom. " 'E's so precious savage a runnin' arter me ! I shall be eaten alive, I knows I shall ! " and with these words he made some frantic clutches at the wall.

"Look out, Tom, here's the dog ! " cried the boys.

"Where ? " cried Tom, who had contrived to dig his nails into a cluster of ivy, to which he held on with the utmost tenacity.

"Close behind you ! "

Tom heard the heavy breathing of the hound, and had only time to let go his hold of the ivy and grasp the rake, when the formidable animal came up to the spot at full swing.

"Now's your time, Tom ! " shouted his friends on the wall, who saw that the grand crisis of the fun was at hand. "Go it, old boy, comb his hair ! cut his claws for him ! "

"It's all werry well to say that, when yer're out o' the way of 'is 'air an' 'is claws ; but just come down 'ere an' see 'ow yer feels yerselves," said Tom reproachfully.

The bloodhound, with bristling back and fierce bloodshot eyes, glared upon Tom, who clung to his rake firmly, as his last and only hope.

The hound crouched for a spring.

"He's coming ! " cried Dick. "Look out, Tom ! "

Tom *did* look out, every way at once.

The dog came, as Dick predicted. His aim was to seize Tom's throat ; but as Tom's neck was so short, there was no throat to seize, consequently his intention was frustrated, and he came to the ground, receiving, as he went, a prog on the back of his head with the sharp teeth of the rake, which sent him howling back to renew the encounter.

Again he crouched.

So did Tom.

The dog sprang up.

Tom bobbed down.

The dog sprang clean over his head.

Tom spun round, and kindly gave him a rub from head to tail with his long-handled comb,

which left a kind of gridiron pattern down Lion's back, drawn in blood.

The brute's savage temper was now thoroughly roused.

"He means it now," cried Dick ; "look at his eyes."

"Stuff the handle down his throat," suggested Harry.

"Don't flurry me," exclaimed Tom, with his round eyes fixed on the bloodhound.

The dog now changed his tactics, and made a snap at the rake.

This manoeuvre Tom frustrated, and returned the compliment by a sharp rap on the nose, which made Lion shake his head and fly madly at Tom's legs and arms.

It was an insane idea on the part of the bloodhound to think of getting either of those members into his mouth, but still he bit with such intensity, that he caught up small portions, little tit bits of Tom's flesh, with such amazing rapidity that Tom felt as though he were being nipped all over with a pair of sharp pliers.

"Oh, oh, oh ! " he cried. " this is wusser an' wusser ! " not forgetting, however, to drop in a blow with the rake whenever he got a chance.

The hound, who seemed to have an instinctive idea that most of the injuries he received came from this instrument, at last, with a determined snap, grasped it in his powerful jaws, and, after a short struggle, wrenched it from Tom's hand.

Tom felt it was all over with him, and seeing the animal growling and gnawing the rake, took advantage of the occasion and bolted at once.

But the hound was not to be cheated of his prey in that manner.

He immediately gave chase, the boys s.houting and saluting him with a volley of plums,

Tom made, with all possible speed for the grape vine that had proved his friend on a former occasion, inwardly execrating himself for not thinking of it before.

But the dog was too quick for him. He had scarcely reached it, when Lion's heavy paws were on his shoulders, and Tom in an instant on his back, with the savage animal standing over him, growling in his face.

"He'll bite my nose off, I know," thought Tom, doubling his fist and literally punching the dog's head, and following up the blow by kicking out with all his might and giving the hound a hoist under his ribs that made him yell.

The contest now took place on the ground, where Tom and the dog rolled over and over in the dust.

Tom, having no other weapon, grasped handfuls of mould, and dashed the soil into the dog's yawning jaws whenever he had the chance.

This seemed the greatest stopper he had yet experienced.

The animal retreated, growled, choked, and sneezed, and gave every token of uneasiness, whilst Tom, profiting by his temporary indisposition, clambered up the wall triumphantly by the vine, which had been firmly nailed up, and was congratulating himself on his fortunate and narrow escape, when, on looking up, he saw, to his extreme horror, the diminutive figure of the dwarf perched on the top of the wall, right in his path.

The pigmy regarded him with an expression of scornful derision, and sat for a moment picking his teeth with the point of his dagger.

"So you thought you'd done for me, did you, eh?" he cried. "You thought you'd cracked my skull, didn't you, and were going to run away after it, didn't you? Ho, ho! Cluck, cluck!" he ejaculated, making a peculiar sharp chirping noise with his mouth.

But Tom had grown rather desperate over his dog fight, and he had got somewhat accustomed to Ghoul's red and green pigs' eyes, and he exclaimed—

"You ain't got no right to stop me. You've set the dorg on to me, an' we've fought it out fair; an' now I wants to be hoff."

"Ho, ho!" laughed the dwarf; "what, go before I've cut your tongue out, and scraped your eyes, and slit your nose, and bored your ears? Oh, no, no!" and with these words, and a hideous yell, he chipped away at Tom's knuckles with the sharp edge of his scimitar.

Tom, who was but mortal, after enduring the chipping for a few seconds, loosed his hold, and dropped into the garden; and at the same moment a brickbat, hurled by Dick from the outside, alighted in the centre of the dwarf's back, and knocked him off the wall. He happened to alight on Tom's shoulders, who looked not unlike Sinbad carrying the old Man of the Mountain.

With great disgust, Tom made a sudden duck with his head; but Ghoul had curled his supple, spindle legs so firmly round Tom's neck that he defied all his efforts to dislodge him.

The hound, too, having emptied his mouth of the dirt, renewed the attack.

Poor Tom, who felt the dwarf's malignant thumb working near his eyes, began to fancy the scraping was going to commence; and what with the tweaks of his nose, the seizures by the hair, the kicks in the ribs, and the progs from the scimitar above, and the nibbling of the dog beneath, he became desperate.

He observed an outhouse at a little distance, towards which he hastily staggered.

A pretty female face with a bright pair of black eyes seemed to be watching him.

This lent him fresh courage.

There was a tank of water near at hand, for watering the garden.

With a sudden effort, he wrenched the dwarf from his position, and, holding him up in his arms for an instant, dashed him into the tank.

The dwarf swore and execrated in some unknown tongue, whilst the bloodhound, by some strange mistake, imagining his prey was going to escape, plunged in after him—whilst Tom, completely tired and done up, staggered to the door, which immediately opened, and allowed him to roll inside, and then immediately closed.

Tom saw that he was regarded complacently by those sparkling orbs, and ejaculating, "Oh, I'm blessed!" in a very indistinct voice, fainted on the floor.

CHAPTER XV.

LADY GODIVA FALLS INTO A TRANCE — THE FATAL NEWS—THE LAST RITES — OTHNIEL'S RESOLVE TO VISIT THE VAULTS—HE SEEKS A COMPANION, AND ACCIDENTALLY FINDS ONE IN PEEPING TOM.

THE Convent of St. Osburg, which had been founded by the Earl of Mercia and the pious Lady Godiva, his wife, was not more than a quarter of a mile distant from the castle.

This proximity had been at the express wish of the countess, who loved to wander in the garden, and cast her eyes upon the sanctuary she had been instrumental in erecting, where the weary heart, tired of the world and its empty follies, might find a safe retreat, till it rested peacefully where life's storms could no longer assail it.

The grey dawn of morning was lighting up the sacred edifice, but even at that early hour the abbess and several of the nuns were assembled in one of the best chambers, where, stretched upon a bed, in a motionless and deathly sleep—though it was not sleep—lay a beautiful female form, enveloped in a mass of golden hair.

It was the Lady Godiva, who, utterly unconscious of the anxious faces by which she was surrounded, lay silent and motionless.

"Will she be spared to us?" anxiously inquired one of the nuns.

"If it be heaven's will, yes," replied the abbess. "The great Ruler of life and death does not permit one of the least of His faithful servants to pass away until his own appointed time."

"But she has been like this so long," answered the young devotee.

"A trance does not always portend death, my child," the abbess answered. "Heaven has, ere now, during the mysterious lethargy of a dreamy state like this, made known its will to the apparently unconscious sleeper. See! even now, as I speak, she begins to wake to life once more. Hush!"

As the abbess ceased speaking, the Lady Godiva opened her eyes, and throwing back the mass of golden tresses by which she was surrounded, gazed dreamily around her.

After some time she appeared to realize her position, and to recognise the features that surrounded her.

She knew she was in the Convent of St. Osburg, and that those who bent over her with such solicitude were friends.

Her eyes gradually became less filmy, and, after a pause, she spoke.

"How long have I been here?" she inquired.

"Four days," replied the abbess.

"Four days," repeated the countess, thoughtfully. "But how came I here—who brought me?" she continued, with an effort at thought, as though memory had but partially returned.

"We heard a faint wail at the convent gate, after the bell had struck the midnight hour," explained the abbess; "and upon opening it we found you lying senseless at the threshold."

"Ah, yes—yes!" the countess exclaimed, with a violent shudder; "I remember all—all now. And this was four days ago?"

" Yes."

The countess closed her eyes and lay back upon her pillow, and seemed disposed to fall once more into her lethargy.

The abbess and the nuns watched her with anxious interest.

She spoke strangely and dreamily.

" I am going on a long journey." were the words that fell from her lips—" a long journey."

The lookers-on gazed in ominous silence at each other.

Presently she opened her eyes and looked scrutinizingly around, but eventually fixed them on the abbess.

" Bid all depart save yourself," she said.

The command was obeyed in silence, and the Lady Godiva and the abbess were alone.

At the end of half-an-hour the abbess left the chamber, locking the door after her.

The nuns eagerly thronged round the superior, with anxious but respectful inquiries after the fair countess, but the abbess at once checked all further questions by the brief sentence—

" *Hush ! she is at rest !*"

*   *   *   *   *

Great grief prevailed at the convent when the report spread of the death of Lady Godiva, and not less was the general mourning throughout the city.

So beautiful, so good, so kind ; every one felt that in her they had lost a sympathizing friend.

Her funeral obsequies were performed with solemn earnestness, and her body placed in the vault beneath the chapel which had been expressly destined for her husband and herself when their earthly course was ended.

But, amongst the numerous mourners for this amiable woman, how felt Othniel, Lord Raven ?

Remorse not repentance raged in his bosom.

He could not but feel within himself that he was guilty.

A voice within him spoke in unmistakeable accents—

" *Thou art the man !* It is thou who hast stricken down this fair flower by thy rude hand."

Then again he cursed the premature rashness of his conduct.

" Had I been more patient," he cried to himself, bitterly ; " in time she might have listened to my suit. Her husband dead, as he will be ere long, she would have looked to me, his friend, for consolation, but now all is lost. I shall never gaze upon that lovely form in its living beauty more."

Thus he reproached himself, and though he felt no true repentance for his crime, he bitterly lamented the treasure his rashness had so rudely deprived him of.

In vain he sought to banish the beautiful countess from his memory.

Sleeping or waking, she seemed ever present. By day his thoughts recalled her; at night, his dreams.

Appalled as he had been at the appearance of the guardian spirit of St. Osburg, in the garden of the castle, he soon persuaded himself with the belief that it was nothing but a phantom of his heated brain, and it speedily passed from his memory.

Not so the image of Godiva.

He pondered upon that so incessantly that at last he became possessed with an unextinguishable desire to gaze once more upon her lovely features, even when shrouded in the frozen rigidity of death.

How was this to be accomplished ?

There was but one way.

The countess lay entombed in the vaults of St. Osburg.

To stand face to face with the dead, he must descend into those solemn precincts.

Should he ?—dare he ?

" Yes !" He dared to descend into the darkest earthly abyss, so that he could find her there, as his reward.

Still, with all his daring, and his strong desire to behold her once again, there was something appalling, even to the most iron nerves, for the destroyer, as he considered himself, to stand face to face with his dead victim.

If he had some confidential friend, or servant who might have accompanied him, such company would have been invaluable ; but there was none.

Even Wolfhart, ignorant and brutal as he was, would have been better than no one.

But he was gone. Where ? With the secret steel of the assassin beneath his mantle; to send the living husband to join his dead wife !

He turned away from the unpleasant thought.

Could he go alone, with no other companion but that most terrible of all to the guilty—his own conscience ?

A voice seemed to answer with a mocking irony—

" No. He dared not, " and Othniel acknowledged to himself, he dared not.

While he was thus cogitating, his ear detected the sound of voices in that department of the castle devoted to the service of the domestics.

He listened.

One voice was Una Brandon's ; but whose was the other ? It was strange to him.

He approached, and the strange voice which came from the throat of our old friend, Peeping Tom, who since the afternoon when Una had opened the door, and received him into the sanctuary of the kitchen, had been seized with a great partiality for paying periodical visits. which happened to be every evening about tea-time, and which period had again come round.

He had devoured an enormous quantity of bread and butter, as he looked in a highly comic and sentimental manner across the tea table at Una's black eyes, and when the repast was finished, he leant back in his chair, placed his two fat hands on his fat knees, and declared " *He didn't know whatever was the matter with him.*"

" You've eaten too much bread and butter, Tom," said Una, with her merry laugh.

But though she laughed then, it may be remarked she had shed many sincere tears at her dear mistress's death, but she had cheered up under the influence of Tom's genial, good-humoured face, and felt on that afternoon as if she could laugh once more.

" Oh no," said Tom, in reply to her remark, seriously, " it ain't the bre'n' butter."

" It's the tea, then ? "

" No, it ain't the tea neither."

" It's because you're getting so fat ? "

"No it ain't," replied Tom, " I've allus been fat, an' it agrees with me very well."

" But it must be *something*," argued Una.

" It *is* somethink ! " returned Tom.

" Do *you* know what it is ? " she inquired, piercing Tom right through and through with a most mischievous look.

" Yes, I does."

" Tell me."

" I don't like."

" Why not ? "

" P'r'aps yer won't be pleased."

" How do you know till you've told me ? "

" That's werry true."

" Tell me—what is it ? "

" It isn't *one* thing, it's *two* things."

" What sort of things ? "

" Round things."

" Plums, Tom. You've eaten two many, you greedy fellow."

" Plums ! " cried Tom, indignantly. "I hav'n't eaten a single plum since—since the last time ; an' that was ever so long ago."

"Do tell me, then," cried Una, a little pettishly. " I'm tired of guessing."

" Well, then, if yer must know," said Tom, "it's them eyes !"

" What eyes ?" asked Una, innocently looking everywhere, as though she expected to see a pair of eyes looking down upon her from the shelves or the ceiling.

" Why, your eyes !" cried the enraptured Tom. " I likes those two black eyes o' yours better than—than gingerbread," he burst out, as though that was the strongest point of comparison he could possibly mention.

Una laughed again at the gingerbread; but Tom had become sentimental, and didn't see anything to laugh at.

" I say, Una, don't keep on a laughin', that's a dear. I don't see as eyes is anythink to make a joke on'."

" I'm not laughing at you," replied Una, laughing still more.

" Oh, you are sich a hout-an-hout pretty gal. I never see anyone to compare with yer. Yer beats Sally Slitherums into fits."

" Sally Slitherums !" echoed Una, with a contemptuous little toss of her head.

" Wouldn't you like to have a sweet'eart, Una ?" continued Tom.

" I could get plenty, if I wanted," answered she.

" There's Lord Othniel's ugly little dwarf—he'd like to make love to me, if I'd let him."

" I should jest like to ketch 'im a making love to yer !" cried Tom, indignantly. " I'd mangle' im! But yer won't let him, will yer ?"

" No, not *him*, most certainly," she replied.

" Nor nobody else ? Nobody but me ;" and having thus expressed himself, he flopped down on his knees in the middle of the kitchen, just as the dark visage of Lord Raven appeared at the door.

The vision of fat Tom Winker kneeling before the pretty Una might, under ordinary circumstances, have awakened a smile upon Othniel's stern features ; but just now his thoughts were far too serious in their nature to admit even that.

Tom's back being towards the door, he was ignorant of his lordship's presence ; but Una was immediately conscious that his eyes were fixed upon them both.

Blushing and frowning prodigiously, she endeavoured to intimate that they were not alone.

But Tom, who flattered himself her blushes were on his account, and who had no suspicion of the real cause, was resolved not to rise from his knees till she had consented to admit him as the beloved of her heart.

" Come now, Una, jest say as I may be your own true lovier—do !" cried Tom, earnestly.

Una blushed more than ever.

" Then," continued Tom, " some day I'll lead yer to the haltar, an' make a Winker on yer. Will yer be a Winker ? Say 'yes '—do be a Winker !"

" Do get up, sir," cried Una, out of patience. " Don't you see his lordship looking at you ?"

" Wheer ?" gasped Tom.

" There," answered Una, pointing to Lord Othniel, who, striding forward, demanded what he wanted there.

Tom glanced over his shoulder, and caught a glimpse of a pair of eyes very different in their expression from Una's, and the effect was so unexpected and startling that Tom, not knowing what to do or where to go, rolled into the cupboard, and sat down, or rather fell down, amongst the pots and pans with a considerable crash.

Una endeavoured to explain the terms of acquaintanceship on which she stood with Tom, and succeeded so far as to satisfy Lord Raven, who nevertheless expressed a hope that so pretty a maiden would never throw herself away on a booby like him.

But this did not reach Tom's ears, inasmuch as, having gorged himself to the full at tea, he laid his head on a log, and went fast off to sleep immediately.

Suddenly, too, an idea fastened upon Lord Raven.

He saw at a glance that Tom was a fool, but this was no bar to his design.

He had rather a partiality for fools, considering they generally had cunning enough to transact his business, without sufficient sense to inquire too closely into it.

With this idea he allowed his features to assume an expression of placidity, and in a bland voice desired Una to summon her enamoured swain from the cupboard.

Una at once obeyed by calling—

" Tom !"

But no answer was returned.

" Tom !—Tom !" she repeated.

A deep snore was audible.

" Oh my !" exclaimed Una — " if he isn't asleep !"

Throwing open the door, there was the ardent lover, snoring away like a prize pig, with his head pillowed on a log.

" Get up !" cried Lord Othniel.

Tom only snored the more.

There was the remains of a large loaf upon the table, his lordship seized it, and with a very good aim, launched it at Tom's head.

" I didn't want any more plums," cried he, rubbing his nob vigorously.

Othniel lost his patience, and advancing to the cupboard seized him by the collar, and almost shook his head off.

"Oh, oh, oh!" roared Tom, aroused from his slumber, "I didn't eat above five or six quarts."

"Rouse yourself, idiot, and stand up," cried Lord Raven.

Tom jumped up in a great state of bewilderment, and stood winking and blinking like an owl in the sun, first at his lordship and then at Una.

"Where are you employed?" inquired Othniel.

"Nowheres," answered Tom.

"Would you be willing to serve me?"

Tom paused a moment, and reflecting that to serve Lord Raven would be to be near Una, declared he would be willing.

The preliminaries were speedily arranged, and when Tom Winker went home that night he electrified his old granny with the news that he was going to be a great man and marry Una Brandon and live up at the castle.

CHAPTER XVI.

THE DARK NIGHT—LORD OTHNIEL FORCIBLY ENTERS THE CHAPEL—THE VAULT OF DEATH —THE DEAD VOICE—TOM GETS THE HORRORS, AND SOMETHING MORE.

THE night was cloudy and obscure, and a cool breeze swept over the face of the sky, when Lord Raven, wrapped in his cloak, left the castle, accompanied by our young friend Peeping Tom.

Various were the emotions that agitated the breast of Othniel Raven.

He was about to enter, forcibly, the sacred edifice, and descend into the dreadful chamber of death.

Tom, who had at that moment no particular emotions of any kind, was occupied in carrying a rude lantern and a crowbar.

Lord Othniel, who looked upon him simply as half an idiot, had, nevertheless, from motives of his own, endeavoured to win his regard, and he had so far succeeded that Tom began to think his lordship was a very agreeable sort of person, without a bit of pride in his composition.

His respect, too, was greatly increased by the favourable manner in which Othniel appeared to regard his aspirations towards Una.

Altogether everything appeared rosy and comfortable, and poor simple Tom felt quite at home—rather too much so, perhaps—with his new master, the first one, by-the-bye, he had ever had.

It was eleven o'clock when they started on this expedition.

It appeared a little mysterious to Tom, going out so late with a lantern and a crowbar, and he puzzled his brains to think whither they were bound.

He remembered having gone out late at night netting sparrows and fishing for eels ; but then they didn't use a crowbar for either of these operations.

He thought there was no harm in just asking the question.

"Where are you going?" he inquired.

"You'll see when we arrive at our destination," was the abrupt reply.

"We're not going a fishin', are we?" he continued, hazarding a second question.

"Fishing!" echoed Othniel. "Fool!"

"They says it's only fools as *does* go a fishing," murmured Tom.

"Silence!" growled Lord Raven, shrouding himself in his cloak. "Pester me with no more questions."

By this time they had arrived at the convent gate.

All was silent ; the inmates appeared to have long since retired to rest.

"Follow me," said Othniel.

They entered the gate and took their course, picking their way between the scattered tomb stones.

"Oh lor'!" said Tom ; "are we going to church?"

Lord Raven either did not hear him, or, if he did, he vouchsafed no reply.

They stopped before the arched door of the chapel.

"Hold the lantern here," said Othniel in a low tone.

Tom did as he was desired.

His master, grasping the iron crowbar, inserted the sharp end into the aperture that divided the folding doors of the old chapel, and moved it to and fro with a persevering, regular motion.

"Oh my heye," said Tom, to himself ; "blest if this 'ere ain't uncommon like burglary. I wonder what he's arter? Well, it ain't no qusiness o' mine."

Una had supplied him with a flask of wine. He took a sip on the sly.

Othniel observed him.

"What have you in that bottle sirrah?" he inquired.

"Physic," answered cunning Tom, with great presence of mind.

"Give it to me : a sudden faintness has seized me," said Othniel.

Tom passed the bottle very unwillingly, and his master drained it to the dregs.

"What pleasant flavoured physic," remarked he.

"What a greedy guts," grumbled Tom.

At last the door, acted upon by the leverage of the crowbar, began to creak, and show signs of yielding.

A few more efforts, and it burst open with a crash.

"Come on," said his lordship, entering.

Tom followed.

They stood within the chapel.

A dead and solemn silence reigned around.

The faint light of the lantern was barely more than sufficient to render the pervading gloom visible.

"'Ow precious dark it is," remarked Tom.

"Hush!" said Othniel.

At this moment, the moon, hitherto obscured, broke from behind the leaden-coloured clouds, and poured her light into the curiously carved windows.

Grim shadows seemed suddenly to fill the chapel.

LADY GODIVA;

OR, PEEPING TOM OF COVENTRY.

THE PROCESSION.

After all, they were but shadows—quaint, indescribable, and exaggerated reflections of carved mouldings and antique cornices, with here and there burlesqued impressions of marble saints in grotesque and unnaturally elongated postures athwart the floor.

Othniel remained for a few moments wrapped in silence, gazing into the gloom, whilst Tom stood looking at nothing particular, inwardly regretting the loss of the contents of his bottle which he had brought with him for his own private and personal accommodation.

"Remain here," said Othniel, whose eyes had now become accustomed to the gloom.

"What! 'ere! all in the dark?" cried Tom, with considerable trepidation in his tone.

"Psha, idiot! What have you to fear?"

"I don't fear nothink ; only I'm allus rayther timorous when I'm standin' over waults where they keeps dead bodies, 'cos of the ghostes," replied Tom.

"They'll do you no harm," answered his master. "Wait here till I return."

With these words, he took up the crowbar and the lantern, and advanced into the body of the building.

"Well," muttered Tom, as his master's footsteps grew fainter in the distance, "this is verry pleasant. I wonder what my old granny ud say if she could see me now ?"

At this moment a bat whirled past and flapped Tom's nose with his wing.

"Oh, lor'! whatever's that ?" he cried, shuddering ; "somethink sharp scraped my nose," rubbing the offended organ, as he spoke, with his knuckles. "I don't like this 'ere place at all."

As he stood casting very suspicious glances round about him, he observed the moonlight streaming through the windows into the side aisles.

"It's a good deal lighter down there," he said to himself ; "I don't see why I should stop in the dark while there's a light to be got ; I shall go there."

In spite, therefore, of Lord Othniel's injunction that he was to remain where he was, he made his way as quietly and as quickly as possible to the side aisle, and seated himself in the snuggest niche he could find. He then comforted himself with a suck at the empty bottle, and then, shutting his eyes, and as an invariable accompaniment, opening his mouth, fell asleep instantaneously.

In the meantime, Othniel had approached the massive tomb reared by the Earl Leofric for the mortal remains of himself and his family.

He placed the lanthern on the ground, for the light was little needed, as the moon bathed the entire space in which he stood in a flood of silver light.

"Here, then," he ejaculated, as he gazed upon the ponderous mausoleum, "lie the remains of the beautiful Godiva. This marble prison holds in its icy jaws all that was once so full of light and loveliness. What phantasy is it that thus prompts me to gaze upon those lineaments now that death's pale seal has stamped them with the signet of corruption? I cannot answer what ; I but obey the irresistible impulse that urges me on. Yes !" he cried, grasping the iron missile, "thou fairest of death's prisoners—thus I unlock your gloomy prison-house."

With these words he directed the point of the crowbar where the ponderous marble slab joined the sides of the tomb.

At this moment a deep sigh fell upon his ear. He started, and listened intently for a moment, in breathless expectation of what was to follow. "Psha !" he cried, as if half ashamed to acknowledge the emotion he experienced, "I am as much a child as that overgrown baby yonder."

Recovering himself, he applied all his strength to raise the stone.

The ponderous mass already cracked and shivered under the influence of the iron lever, when again he was brought to a stand by the sound of a voice.

It fell upon his ear like some weird strain of music ; though sweet, it was so deep and solemn, as it uttered the command—

"Forbear !"

"Who speaks ?" cried Othniel, the cold drops bedewing his forehead.

"Look upon me," cried the voice.

Lord Othniel Raven, as if spellbound, mechanically directed his gaze towards the spot whence the sound proceeded, when, with a mingled feeling of pleasure, surprise mingled with awe, he beheld the form of Lady Godiva, the object of his thoughts and desires, clad in the white robes of the dead, and looking more spiritually beautiful than ever in the pale moonlight.

Her lips moved.

"Wouldst thou, with sacrilegious hand, disturb her repose, whose honour thou wouldst have blurred while living? Begone, lest the vengeance of heaven overtake thee here, and thou be not suffered to leave this sacred spot alive !"

Othniel, awe-struck and bewildered, had lost his usual presence of mind and audacity, as he stood thus face to face with the incorporeal, and was unable to reply.

The spirit continued in the same solemn strain.

"You may harm the living, but the dead you cannot injure—they are beyond your power."

As she uttered these words, she appeared to retreat with a slow, gliding motion. Her calmbright eyes, stern in their repose, still fixed upon the nobleman, who, as rigid as the statues that surrounded him, still gazed at her in silence.

At last she disappeared entirely, and Othniel, pale and unnerved, sank down upon the marble steps that led up to the tomb.

It was at this juncture that our worthy friend Tom Winker awoke from his forty winks, with a slight sensation of chilliness.

"Oh !" said he, shuddering, "isn't it cold ?" taking at the same time another pull from the empty bottle. "Ah !" he grumbled, "if that guts of a lord hadn't a gone and emptied it there'd a been enough for me now. I wonder whatever 'e's a doin' of down there so long ? P'raps a ghost's got 'old of 'im by the leg."

As he gave utterance to this suggestion, he peered anxiously down the aisle; not that he was particularly concerned about his master's fate, only the idea struck him that it might occur to the ghosts, after finishing with his lordship, to come and give him a turn.

His sensations may therefore be imagined when, with this pleasing idea prominent in his mind, he saw in the distance a ghostly form slowly approaching.

Tom looked—it was all he could do—motion was out of the question. His knees knocked together, and his feet seemed glued to the ground; his rosy chubby cheeks became suddenly blanched; what hair he was possessed of (it was not much) stood on end like bristles, and his teeth played an involuntary solo, like a pair of castanets.

"Oh lor ! oh dear ! Is it a comin' 'ere ?" he groaned inwardly.

There was no doubt of it; it was coming. There was no other way for it to come.

"I shall be gobbled up alive, I knows I shall,

an' granny 'ull never know what's become of me. Oh, what a wicked boy I am!"

Tom had a conscience, and, whenever he was in trouble, the said conscience gave him awful digs.

"What shall I do?" he continued, whimpering. "I n-n-n-never c-c-could abide g-g-g-ghostes! Oh, ain't it white! It's been a eatin' 'is lordship, an' now it's a comin' to eat me. Oh, won't it 'ave a rich lick!"

And as the spectre approached, and the prospect became every moment more and more critical, our gallant friend Tom plumped down on his knees and hid his fat face in his fat hands, keeping, however, at the same time a sharp look out between his fingers.

Still onwards glided the ghost, and so short a distance now intervened between them, that our worthy friend's terror could no longer be controlled.

He had not lost the use of his vocal organs, in proof of which he roared at the top of his voice—

"Murder! m-m-murder! Lord What's-your-Name, here's the ghost of a—a—thing-a-my! It's a female ghost, an' she's a comin' to eat me up alive! M-murder! m-m-murder!"

The dread spirit was now within a few yards of the terrified Tom when she suddenly paused, and in a voice at once gentle and assuring, said—

"You need fear nothing from me. I will not harm you." And disappeared through a small door in the wall, which Tom had not previously noticed.

"Phew!" exclaimed our corpulent friend, as the door closed upon the spirit. "I never was so 'orrified in all my life—never!"

The cries of Peeping Tom had the effect of arousing Othniel from the lethargy into which he had sunk as the form of Godiva disappeared from his sight.

The earthly sounds restored him, and he started up from his recumbent posture, his dark eyes flashing with anger as he listened to the yells of his follower.

"What's the matter with the fool," he muttered to himself, "that he thus startles the night with his cries?"

Without waiting to indulge in further surmise as to the cause of the alarm, he hastily strode to the spot where he had left the worthy Tom. Tom, however, was nowhere to be found.

"Where has the idiot strayed to?" growled Othniel, branching off and proceeding along the side aisle. "I wish now I had performed this errand alone; the cries of that booby are enough to wake the dead."

At this juncture he stumbled over some bulky substance in his path, and fell prostrate.

It is almost needless to add that the bulky substance alluded to was the luckless Tom Winker, who was coiled up in a heap, nose and knees together, hardly daring to look up, much less to move.

"Oh my—— Oh! oh!" groaned Tom, as the sharp toe of the noble came into painful contact with a certain part of his anatomy in which he was particularly sensitive.

"What in the fiend's name have we here?" shouted Othniel, regaining his feet instantly in no very amiable temper.

"It's only me," murmured Tom, mildly.

"Why, then, hast thou made this infernal uproar?"

"I thought as I saw a ghost all in white."

"Psha! Ghost indeed!" cried his master, with angry contempt. "You've been asleep and dreaming, or your dull brains are muddled with wine."

"I'm sure they ain't," replied Tom, with energy. "You took care of that; you emptied my bottle."

"Silence, sirrah!" And as he spoke he hoisted Tom from the ground with a jerk, that set him shaking all over like a jelly.

"Now let us begone!" cried his lordship, striding to the door rapidly. "Come!"

Tom came as he was ordered, and followed his impetuous master as he walked rapidly forward towards the castle.

CHAPTER XVII.

PEEPING TOM BEGINS TO FIND HIMSELF AT HOME AT THE CASTLE—HE VISITS HIS OLD FRIENDS, AND BRINGS HOME A STOCK OF PINS—MEETS A VEILED MONK, AND RECEIVES A LETTER AND A PURSE—GHOUL COMMITS A ROBBERY, AND IS CAUGHT—THE LETTER GETS INTO WRONG HANDS—A BRAWL, AND THE RESULT—TOM IN PRISON.

PEEPING TOM was becoming accustomed to the routine of his daily life at the castle. True, there were some difficulties to surmount—a great many difficulties. There was the lord of the castle, the dark-browed, swarthy-visaged Othniel; then there came the sallow, sinister Doctor Antonio Crux, an Italian physician, who ministered to the bodily ailments of all who needed it, and who looked with an eye of suspicion at Tom whenever he passed him, as though he longed to bleed him. After this worthy came the ugly dwarf Ghoul, with his unnaturally large head and his spindle legs, and last, not least, his malevolent, spiteful temper. And in addition to these a troop of Norman soldiers, with the addition of several Dutch mercenaries, to whom Tom's punchy figure and his other peculiarities afforded an incessant fund of amusement.

But Tom was a philosopher, or perhaps—and this may be nearer the truth—he was by no means thin-skinned.

When Nature turned him into the world a fat, awkward, good-natured simpleton, she acted wisely in not giving him a larger supply of brains than was absolutely necessary.

She, however, made up for the deficiency by endowing him with an excellent appetite, and this went a long way towards keeping our worthy friend's temper in a proper state of equilibrium.

No matter what happened to ruffle him in the course of the morning—no matter the insults, sarcasms, nay blows, that were inflicted on him before dinner—all were forgotten long before the termination of the daily meal, and Tom might have been seen, with mouth extended from ear to ear, laughing with all his might in company, and in perfect good fellowship with those who an hour or two before were goading, or rather trying to goad, him to the verge of madness.

But Tom was becoming inured to his position, and the frowns of his master, the ominous glances of the physician, the spite of the dwarf, and the practical jokes of the soldiers, were beginning to lose their power, and to be looked upon as matters of course.

Certainly the ill-grained Ghoul did try Tom's patience more than all the rest.

He seemed to live for the express purpose of spying out Tom's actions, and hardly any event happened either for or against him but there was Ghoul on the spot, as though he had dropped from the clouds, with his shrill malicious scream, or his ironical "Ho! ho!" either to mar his triumph or to add to his discomfort.

But then, to counterbalance this, there was pretty Una, who regarded Tom with an eye of particular favour, and who, though herself of the neatest and most symmetrical proportions, saw nothing absurd or ridiculous in Tom's squat figure, or the excessive development of his legs. So that, all things considered, Tom looked upon himself as perfectly happy,

It was a lovely summer's morning when Tom was despatched with a mission to the good town of Coventry.

He had performed his duty, and popped into his old granny's cottage, who had, in duty bound, washed his face till it shone like the rising sun, and brushed his hair till he felt red-hot; and, in return for the infliction, presented him with a fabulous supply of gingerbread, which he stowed away in his pocket, and hastened off to hunt up his old friends, the boys; which, having done, they adjourned to the tavern in the Market-place, and there, over a flagon of Bungs' very best, recounted past adventures, and vowed unchanging friendship for the future.

The flagon being emptied, his companions accompanied him a considerable distance on his road back to the castle, and then, having embraced him so warmly that he was fain to cry out "Hold, enough!" they left him.

Tom was in the best of tempers.

The gingerbread he had eaten had satisfied his appetite, and the ale he had drank had warmed his heart and raised his spirits.

Still, as he drew near the chapel that had been the scene of his last recorded adventure, he became painfully conscious of sharp, shooting pains in the calves of his legs, and other localities that we need not dwell upon.

"It's werry funny," said he to himself, stopping and writhing slightly. "Whatever can it be as gives me sich prickin' pains in my legs? I could almost fancy as I'd got the pins an' needles in 'em. P'raps I've overwalked myself, an' my muscles is contracted? I'll sit down an' rest myself."

As he came to this resolution, he suited the action to the word, and plumped down on the grass without further deliberation, but sprang up again with the swiftness of a Jack-in-the-box, clapping his hand behind him in a most excited manner.

"Oh! oh! oh!" he cried. "There's no mistake about that—'tis pins, as sure as my name's Tom Winker!"

Had he been less engrossed in this discovery, he might have heard a suppressed giggle, and have noticed his loving but mischievous friends enjoying the joke behind an adjacent hedge.

"They is pins!" he ejaculated, as, after a deliberate and careful manipulation of his hind quarters, he drew forth six of those useful, but, under the above circumstances, highly irritating articles.

"Them boys ha' done this. The hidear o' their a makin' a pincushion o' my posterities; an' I shouldn't wonder if there wasn't some in my legs as well."

He accordingly submitted those members to a rigid ocular investigation.

"Yes," he cried suddenly. "My calves is a reg'lar pincushion. Well, I never! One, two, three, four, five, six, seven, eight. No wonder I felt prickin' sensations," he continued, as he extracted the pins, "nine, ten—such big 'uns, too—eleven, twelve. Oh! here's a whopper,—thirteen."

The mischievous boys in the meantime rolled on the ground with delight at Tom's philosophical calculation, half suffocated with their efforts to restrain their risible faculties.

"Wait till I see 'em again," cried Tom, "I'll jest tell 'em what I think. I'm as full o' holes as a pepper castor."

"Ho! ho! ho!" laughed a harsh, screaming voice, which he recognised as the dwarf's, "there's a pincushion."

Tom looked round, but the small individual was not to be seen.

"Ah! you may laugh, you little, undersized lump o' nothink," shouted Tom, indignantly. "Never mind, I'll make a pincushion o' you some day."

Still his concealed tormentor did not appear, and Tom—the irritation of the pins having partly subsided—was about to proceed on his journey, when a figure, shrouded in a monk's gown and cowl, drawn over the head so as entirely to conceal his features, touched him lightly on the shoulder.

Tom turned and stopped.

"*Benedicite!*" said the monk, in a sweet, calm tone.

"Thankee," replied Tom, "same to you, an' many of 'em."

"You look like an honest fellow," continued the mysterious figure.

"I 'opes as I'm as honest as other people," returned Tom.

"Honester than most, I trust, or I shall fear to employ you," answered the other.

"Don't be afeard o' me. When I says I does anythink, I does it," said Tom, decidedly.

"Do you know Shadow Wood?" inquired the monk.

"Do I? Don't I? I've got chesnuts and hunted squirrels there times out o' number."

"Can I trust you with this letter?"

"O' course you can."

"Take it, then, and go at once to the entrance of the wood. There you will meet a man wearing a grey friar's dress. He will say to you two words, '*For her.*' You will answer 'Yes,' and you will place that letter in his hand."

The monk, as he spoke, placed the missive in Tom's hand.

"Guard it, as you would your life. It is a matter of life and death importance," he continued, "and accept this as your reward," tendering as he spoke a small purse well filled with gold.

Tom, in whose brains visions of joyous revelry immediately floated, promised to perform his errand faithfully, and in a few moments he was once more alone—the monk had disappeared.

"A puss full o' gold for deliverin' a letter," cried the delighted simpleton. "What a generous monk, an' what a white hand he'd got! Well, as I've been paid in advance, I'll take it at once. I can get back by dinner time."

He accordingly put the letter in the pouch he carried by his side, and set off upon his mission.

He had not gone many yards when he heard steps behind him, and looking round he was by no means agreeably surprised to see the thin legs and wrinkled yellow visage of Ghoul the dwarf.

"Good morning, my dear friend," cried the dwarf, in a tone that was meant to be insinuating, but so harsh and unpleasant that it struck upon the ear like the croaking of a raven; "you walk so fast I can hardly keep up with you."

"I don't want you to keep up with me," replied Tom. "I'm in a hurry."

"In a hurry," returned the dwarf; "that's strange. I never knew you to be in a hurry before."

"Well, then, you know it now," said Tom, in a tone of annoyance; "so don't bother me, or I shall put my foot upon you, an' scrunch yer!"

The dwarf, who at another time would have screeched out a defiance at such a threat, now took no notice of it, but said, in a wheedling tone—

"I know your errand. You're going to deliver a letter to a friar at the entrance of Shadow Wood. I saw the monk give it you, and a purse of gold as well."

"I am," said Tom, boldly; "and what then?"

"Oh, nothing," answered Ghoul, "only I should like to look at the letter before you deliver it."

"Don't yer wish yer may get it?" replied Tom. "What's it got to do with you?"

"Oh, certainly, it's nothing to me, only I'm curious to look at it."

"Then you may put your curiosity in your pocket, 'cos yer ain't a goin' to 'ave a sight of it!"

He had hardly delivered himself of this brief speech when he stumbled over something, and pitched on his nose.

The something that led to this result was the dwarf's foot, which he adroitly thrust out as he walked by Tom's side, and which led to the overthrow of the latter.

Tom groaned over his damaged nose, whilst the dwarf was profuse in his apologies as he gave him a hand up, and in a most officious manner, chuckling all the time with delighted malice, flapped the dust out of Tom's garments with his hand.

"That'll do," said Tom, rather sulkily, "an' now don't follow me any more;" and with this admonition he once more sallied forwards.

He had not gone half a dozen steps when the well-known voice of Dare Devil Dick fell upon his ear.

"I say, Tom," it cried, "that ugly humpty-dumpty pigmy's got your letter."

"What!" cried Tom, thrusting his hand into his pocket, and missing not only the letter but the purse of gold; "so he has, an' the purse as well."

This was a fact. The dwarf, as soon as his corpulent friend measured his length on the ground, thrust his hand adroitly into the leathern satchel at Tom's side and abstracted its contents, with which he was now hurrying to the castle as fast as his small legs could carry him.

"Stop 'im!" shouted Tom; "stop the dialogical willin'!"—he meant diabolical—"after him, boys!"

The boys needed no second appeal, and uttering a loud yell, they set off at full speed, like a troop of hunters after a monkey.

The dwarf ran, and they ran; but in the race the former had no chance. In a few moments he was in the hands of his pursuers, who hoisted him off his legs as they would have done a cat or a rabbit, and seemed very much inclined to disjoint him.

"Wring 'is ugly neck, the purloinin' wagabones!" cried Tom, who came up puffing and blowing like a grampus.

"Let's have a game at catch ball with him first," sung out Dare Devil Dick.

"Ay, ay," echoed the boys, Tom included, who, with the easiness of temper that was natural to him, had almost forgotten his loss, and was grinning at the prospect of the fun.

"Now, then," said Dick, "all ready. One! two! three!" and away flew the diminutive culprit to Quicksilver Harry, who caught him, and pitched him to Quiet Will, who transferred him to Sleepy Joe, who dropped him, and picked him up again by his foot.

Ghoul swore, spit, spluttered, and fizzed like an angry cat, and what would have been the termination of the affair is more than doubtful, had not his cries aroused the three Brabançons, who were playing at dice in the court-yard, and who immediately ran out to the rescue.

Ghoul, catching a glimpse of them, jerked himself out of Joe's hand, and set off at full speed to meet his friends, followed by the boys.

The mercenaries—Karl, Wilhelm, and Johann—whom our readers will remember on a previous occasion in the market-place, interposed between the pursuers and the pursued, who, finding himself in a position of safety, stopped at the castle gate, and, holding up the letter and the purse in his clenched hand, shook them derisively with a hoarse laugh, and having performed this feat, ran through the gates into the arms, or rather between the legs of Lord Othniel, who gave him a kick which sent him back with a rebound, rolling over like a football, and causing him to drop both letter and purse.

"What is this?" cried his lordship, possessing himself of both the prizes, and, pocketing the latter, the jingle of which was an answer to his question, as he examined the former.

Ghoul, having picked himself up, looked ruefully at his master's proceedings without daring to offer any objection, and at once came to the conclusion that as there was no prospect of his sharing in the plunder, he might as well make a virtue of necessity, and take the credit for zeal in his master's service.

Othniel stood gazing at the superscription on the letter with a thoughtful expression on his features. He recognised in the delicate characters the handwriting of Lady Godiva.

The address was as follows :—

To the
Reverend Mother in God,
The Abbess of St. Mary's Convent,
Paris.

"What does this mean ?" soliloquized Othniel, in an under tone. "How came this in your possession ?" he inquired suddenly of the dwarf.

"I'll tell your noble lordship," answered that personage. " I saw Tom Winker receive it from a monk, who told him to deliver it to a grey friar, who was waiting for it at the entrance of Shadow Wood. This friar was to say two words, " *For her,*" and Tom was to answer ' *Yes,*' and then he was to give the letter. He received the purse also "——

"Never mind the purse," said Othniel, abruptly ; "begone !"

The dwarf vanished, grumbling spitefully as he went at the cool appropriation of his spoils by his master.

"Never mind !" he muttered, "never mind ! I'll have it out of that fat-headed fool !"

No sooner had Ghoul disappeared than Lord Othniel, as the shortest plan of arriving at the intention of the letter, broke the seal, and read the contents. It ran thus :—

" REVERED MOTHER,—You may look upon this letter as coming from the grave, and the words of the dead are sacred. It is of my daughter I would speak, my beloved Algitha. You, who have a mother's heart for all mankind, will understand my anxiety on her account, though I feel, under your care, she is safe. She is young, beautiful ; guard her, cherish her, and, on no account, suffer her to leave the calm and holy sanctuary, where the arrows of the wicked and the sorrows of the world cannot reach her. I shall depart in peace, knowing the arms of your affection are around her.

Yours, Holy Mother, in love and duty,
                    GODIVA."

" So," said Othniel to himself, " this letter must have been written, then, before she died." He paused thoughtfully, and then continued, slowly—"Algitha is beautiful, more beautiful, perhaps, than her mother, if that be possible. Why should not she fill up the void that her mother's death has left in my breast ? I must think—I must think," and, with contracted brow, compressed lips, and arms folded across his breast, he paced moodily to and fro.

His meditations were suddenly interrupted by a confused sound of yells and execrations without the walls.

Othniel started, annoyed at this sudden breaking in upon his guilty thoughts, and as the confusion still continued, he hastily went forth from the gates.

The sight that greeted him did not tend to subdue his irritability.

The three Dutchmen were surrounded by the troop of boys, who stuck to them like leeches. Their daggers had been long since perforce relinquished by the blows of the cudgels on their knuckles, which were swollen and contused by the vigorous raps they had received.

In short, to sum the matter up in a few words, they were getting decidedly the worst of it.

It was in vain they hustled, and hugged, and wrestled ; on every side blows fell like hail, until wounded, bruised, and bleeding, the three mercenaries could neither offer any effectual resistance or retaliation, and, what was worse, they could not even escape.

It was at this crisis that Othniel came upon the scene, and the sight of his men thus beset roused him to fury.

Winding a blast upon the horn that hung at his side he rushed forward, and, almost simultaneously, a body of armed soldiers appeared at the castle gates.

Dare Devil Dick, who caught sight of them, and whose arm was tired of hitting, whispered to his friend Harry, "It's time to be off ; " and this intimation having been passed round, by the time Othniel reached the spot the only occupants were the three damaged Brabançons and Tom Winker, who, feeling himself an injured party, stood his ground.

"What is the meaning of this brawl, knaves ? " he cried, fiercely, glancing from one to the other.

Tom proceeded to explain, with considerable energy, the circumstances that led to it ; but so far from eliciting any sympathy, he was considerably chagrined to find himself suddenly checked, and to hear the command of his master uttered in a tone of impatient irritability—

" Take this idiot away, and lock him up."

The order was instantly obeyed, and the whole party returned to the castle.

The last sound that greeted Tom's ears ere he was placed in confinement, was the mocking, discordant laugh of the dwarf, and the last sight his eyes beheld was his puckered and vindictive features, and his malignant eyes fixed upon him, gleaming with hatred and revenge.

CHAPTER XVIII.

THE FORGED LETTER AND ITS CONSEQUENCES—ALGITHA AND HER CONFIDANTE—THE GUARDIAN AND HIS WARD—A MOMENT OF PERIL—A WELL-TIMED SHOT—THE WARNING.

OTHNIEL, after brooding upon the letter, resolved in his evil heart to make it subservient to the accomplishment of the designs that it had caused to spring up in his breast.

His strong, passionate, and licentious nature was stirred fiercely within him, as his thoughts wandered to the beautiful Algitha, whom he had not seen since she was a mere child, but whom he felt convinced must inherit the charms of her mother.

Under this impression, he set himself to forge a letter in as exact imitation of Lady Godiva's hand as possible, of an entirely different purport, summoning Algitha to return home at once.

This letter was delivered by one of his own followers, to the grey friar, who was at the appointed spot waiting its arrival, and the result of the missive was that in the course of a few weeks the fair girl was an inmate once more of the home of her childhood, and under the guardianship of the licentious and unprincipled Lord Othniel.

* * * * * *

The sun was shining brightly, and darting his beams into the chamber set apart for the use of Algitha.

Its occupants were the fair maiden herself and the pretty Una, who had been appointed her waiting-maid, to the great delight of the latter.

There was something wondrously winning, not only in the beauty of Algitha but also in her manner and the sound of her voice, and Una rejoiced at the privilege of being permitted to attend upon one so beautiful and so good. Hers was, indeed, a service of love.

But though all nature was smiling, a sadness rested on the fair face of Algitha.

She inherited her mother's beauty in some points, though the resemblance between them was not striking.

She was less tall, and lacked the magnificent proportions of limb that characterized the Lady Godiva; but then she was not yet seventeen, and resembled the delicate bud just opening its beauties to the dawning spring, whilst her mother was the gorgeous blossom glowing in the summer sun.

Still there was the magnificent golden tresses, and the expressive, violet blue eyes, beaming with love, and that delicately-rounded bodily conformation, that promised, as she grew older, all that a poet or a painter would desire to immortalise, either on canvas or in verse.

Othniel, at the first sight of her, was enchanted,—dazzled; but as her lovely eyes glanced at him, and her silver voice fell on his ear, he became fairly intoxicated beneath their potent spell.

She now sat with her head resting on her hand, and her fair tresses sweeping in dishevelled loveliness over her shoulders, listlessly gazing upon vacancy, whilst ever and anon a deep sigh stole forth involuntarily, revealing in its own peculiar and significant manner that the heart was not quite at rest within.

Una had observed the abstraction of her young mistress and heard her sighs, and began to be full of sympathy, though for what, she did not know.

At last this sympathetic feeling became too powerful to be controlled, and, as Algitha sighed once more for the sixth time, Una remarked—

"Oh, my dear mistress, I'm sure you must be very unhappy; you do nothing but sigh."

"I am not very happy, Una," was the mild reply.

"And you, too, so good, so beautiful, to be unhappy! It's too bad, that it is," continued the little maiden.

"I have heard say that all who come into this world are born to trouble. Therefore, neither goodness nor beauty are exempt from it," said Algitha, somewhat sadly.

"I do love you, dear lady!" burst out Una, with a sudden energy that almost startled her mistress. "Yes, I love you, though I've only known you a few weeks, and it breaks my heart to see you so melancholy when you ought to be as happy as the day is long. Ah! if I were your sister, instead of your waiting maid, I should throw my arms round your neck, and ask you to let me share your sorrow, whatever it might be."

There is something about genuine sympathy that invites, and generally gains confidence. It was so in this instance; for the young beauty drew the kind-hearted domestic to her and kissed her rosy cheek.

"Kind girl," she said, "whatever be the grief from which I suffer, it will rejoice you to know that your sympathy is at least some alleviation."

"Is it though, really?" exclaimed the delighted Una. "Oh, I am glad, very glad; and I think, if you would not be angry, I could guess what it is that makes you unhappy."

"Do you think so?"

"I am almost sure I could. There's only one thing in the world can make a young girl of sixteen or seventeen really unhappy, at least in my opinion."

"And what is that?" inquired Algitha.

"Love!" answered Una, boldly; "that is, when I say love, I mean unrequited love, of course."

"That is not the cause of my sadness," said Algitha, with another sigh.

"Oh, no, I never thought it was," cried the young domestic, with energy, "so beautiful as you are"——

"Hush, hush, Una," said her mistress, reprovingly. "You must not talk so much about my beauty. I had no hand in producing it, and have, therefore, nothing to be proud of in its possession."

"But I can't help talking of it," continued Una, with excited volubility, "I should like to see any one in the world that could refuse to love you."

"They might be found many such," answered Algitha, "though I confess I have not experienced much unkindness hitherto."

"But," Una went on, "there is another sorrow attached to love that I haven't spoken of, though I was coming to it, and that is separation from the one we love, and who loves us better than all the world."

Algitha started; tears came into her eyes— Una had touched the right chord.

"That is my case," she said.

"Oh, how I do pity you!" cried Una, "and the poor dear young gentleman, how wretched he must be. I pity him as well, poor fellow!"

"I am sure he will miss me; he will feel my loss, I believe, as deeply as I deplore his, dear Rupert!"

"Rupert," echoed Una, "what a pretty name! and I dare say the owner is pretty, too."

"I never saw anyone yet half so handsome," said Algitha, sighing again; and so one word led on to another, till at length the young beauty opened her heart to her faithful servant, and poured into her attentive ear the full history of her love. How she had first seen Rupert at mass on a Sunday—how their eyes had met—and how, having met, they found it difficult to separate them, or to withdraw their thoughts from earth, to raise them heavenward. She recounted how that, one day, when she was fearing she might never see him more, he suddenly appeared beneath the convent window, gazing upon her with eyes that spoke love's silent but unmistakeable language; how they subsequently met, and that she then discovered he was of noble birth, though for some reason compelled to live abroad as a physician, ignorant even of his legitimate name and title.

All this deeply interested Una, who drank in with avidity every word that fell from the lips of her mistress.

"You saw each other before you left, did you not?" she inquired, eagerly.

"Oh, yes!" answered Algitha, "and exchanged our vows, and plighted our troths to each other; but yet," sadly continued the young girl, "it seems such a long, dreary interval ere we shall meet again."

Una tried to cheer her as far as she was able, and having arranged her mistress's rebellious locks, and encircled them with a band of pearls, she left her to seek out Tom, who had been in close confinement for some days, and who was only released at her special intercession.

Lord Othniel had an eye for beauty, and Una was a beauty after her fashion, and it was to this fact her influence over her sensual master may be attributed.

She had hardly departed, when Algitha received a message from Othniel, desiring her presence.

She at once prepared to obey, and first glancing in the mirror and catching a glimpse of a face and form beautiful enough to have caused a second siege of Troy, descended to meet her guardian.

Lord Othniel was charmed with her appearance, her voice, and her conversation.

All that she said, all that she did, conspired to increase his admiration, and add fresh fuel to the flame that consumed him.

To the inquiries Algitha made after her parents Othniel informed her of her noble father's destination, and as an excuse for her mother's absence, invented an excuse that she was gone to do penance at the shrine of some distant city, and to pray for the earl's safe return.

This satisfied the unsuspecting girl, and she would soon have felt at home with her guardian, had he not of his own headlong precipitation, both alarmed and disgusted her ere the first strangeness of their meeting had worn away.

"You have been too long away, beautiful Algitha," he exclaimed, fixing his dark piercing eyes, full of unholy fire, upon the fair cheek that the ardour of his gaze suffused with blushes.

"I had grown accustomed to the quiet retreat of St. Mary's Convent, and was very happy there," she answered, almost at a loss for a reply.

"It shall not be my fault if you are not much happier here," replied the enamoured Othniel, who could hardly restrain his desire to throw himself at her feet. "You have been hitherto so immured, that the delights that the world offers to youth and loveliness like yours, are unknown to you, and unappreciated, because as yet untasted. It shall be my task to guide your feet into the path where the atmosphere is ever fragrant with Love's sweet blossoms, if you will accept my companionship."

"I shall always consider it my duty to look up to him whom my parents consider worthy to take charge of their child," was Algitha's answer.

"Your duty? Yes," said Othniel, somewhat chilled by the coldness of her tone; "but I should be happier if your inclinations went hand in hand with that duty."

"That which at first is duty *may* in time become inclination," she answered.

"It may, it will, it shall!" said Othniel, starting up and throwing himself at her feet, whilst with his arm he encircled her waist. "It is here, at your feet, I would break down the cold icy barrier of duty, that I may press you to my heart, and tell you I worship, I adore you!" and as he spoke he drew her closer to him.

Astonishment, surprise, and disgust at this glaring breach of decorum kept Algitha for a moment speechless.

She remained gazing at the swarthy visage and the gleaming eyes that were upturned towards hers.

Othniel misinterpreted her manner and her look for the indecision of a weak mind, but she soon undeceived him.

Suddenly starting up, she flung his hand from her, as though its very touch had been pollution.

"Lord Othniel, for shame!" she cried, her fair face, brow, and neck crimson with indignation. "Is it thus you guard the sacred treasure confided to your trust? Think you my parents would thank the man who, under the character of guardian would prove the destroyer of their child? Allow me to retire; I can no longer speak to you."

She made her way towards the door as she spoke; but this was the very last result Othniel either desired or anticipated. He was, moreover, piqued at the evident aversion she expressed towards him, not only in words, but in her manner; and from being the applicant, he became transformed into the commander.

"Stay!" he cried. "I have done nothing more than assure you of the devotion I feel towards you. If to love you, to assure you of that love be a crime, then I am guilty; but if, on the other hand, the honest avowal of a true affection be that which the best and greatest in the land may make their boast of, I repudiate the charge of guilt, and candidly confess a passion I am proud to feel."

"Then let me at once assure you that passion is hopeless. I cannot give you my heart, simply because I have none to give. If there were no other reasons, that would be decisive."

"You love another, then?"

"I do."

"And do you imagine that when Othniel Raven loves as he loves you, he is prepared in an instant to discard all his cherished ideas? If so, you know me not."

"I think I do—I fear I do," said Algitha, "for a wicked, deceitful man, utterly unfit to be the guardian of any one less guilty than yourself."

"Psha!" cried Othniel, maddened at her reproof. "You speak like a child that has never yet been out of its nursery. But, say—think—do what you like. I have told you that I love you, and whether you return me love or scorn in exchange, I am equally resolved to be your master. Reflect; is it worth a struggle, when we might be so peaceable and happy? Ask yourself the question."

"I have done so, and whatever *your* creed may teach on that point, mine tells me that even war in a just cause, is preferable to an inglorious peace. You threaten me. Well, let there be war between us—hatred—anything but love!"

With these words she was about hastily to quit the room, when, as if divining her intent, he followed her, and placed his hand upon her wrist.

"Not so fast!" he cried; "there is no escape, the door is locked."

"Would you dare detain me in my own father's castle a prisoner? I will appeal to all within its walls for protection!" she exclaimed indignantly,

"No doubt you would," returned Othniel, with a grim smile, "if you had the opportunity; but that you may rest assured you will not have."

"What mean you?" she exclaimed with violent indignation.

"I mean," replied her disagreeable, or rather brutal lover, "that you are here in my safe custody, and here you will remain.

Algitha, terrified at his violence, struggled to escape, but in vain.

The very effort she made seemed to increase the certainty of her thraldom, till at last her loud screams pierced through the massive walls of the apartment, and reached the ears of Una and Tom, who were making love quietly in their own way, in the lower part of the castle.

They immediately hastened to Lord Othniel's apartment; but when they reached the door, all was silent. The screams had ceased, and they returned under the impression their ears had deceived them.

All was silent.

The beautiful and helpless maiden no longer shuddered or struggled, she no longer uttered a cry for help—she had fainted, and now hung like a drooping lily, beaten down by the tempest, quite passively in the arms of her ruthless assailant.

"She is mine!" he shouted; "this beautiful, this dainty treasure, mine—mine! The mother escaped me, but the daughter's presence atones for her loss;" and gazing upon her lovely form with gloating, fiery eyes, he kissed her passionately—and repeatedly he had passed that point beyond which reason, prudence, or religion have power to check or to control. The fate of the helpless Algitha had arrived at a climax; her doom was to all appearance sealed, when an arrow came crashing through the window, and passing in its flight in close proximity to the guilty ravisher, buried its barbed point in the wall of the chamber.

Othniel started at this unexpected visitation, and depositing his helpless burden on a couch, advanced to the spot where the fragile weapon still quivered in its resting-place.

After a moment's pause, he drew it forth, and the colour fled from his cheek, as his eye fell upon the ominous words distinctly traced upon the missile—BEWARE THE GREY MONK!

CHAPTER XIX.

ALGITHA RECOVERS HER SENSES, BUT BECOMES AN INVALID—DR. CRUX PRESCRIBES UNSUCCESSFULLY—A STORMY NIGHT—THE CRY FOR HELP—THE BENIGHTED WANDERER—DR. CRUX GIVES THE TRAVELLER SHELTER, AND DISCOVERS A KINDRED SPIRIT.

THE reading of this threat, or rather warning, produced a sudden and marked effect upon the guilty Othniel.

He stood for some moments with his eyes riveted upon the shaft of the arrow, contemplating the ominous characters with an expression of bewildered conjecture.

Then, having placed the weapon in a cabinet, he strode to the couch, where the prostrate Algitha, who had not yet recovered from the deep swoon into which her terror had cast her, lay motionless and apparently lifeless.

"I have been too hasty!" he cried. "I have allowed my delicate prey to see the snare I would cast around her; she has taken alarm, and will now be more difficult than ever to entrap."

It was with this idea prominent in his mind that he unlocked the door; and, summoning Una to assist him, coolly informed her that her young mistress had been suddenly seized with a fainting fit, and must be removed to her chamber.

Having made this disclosure, he took up the fair burden in his arms, and, followed by Una, carried her to her own apartment, where he left her to go in search of Doctor Crux, whose services appeared particularly necessary to rouse her once more into consciousness.

*   *   *   *   *

Some weeks had passed away. It was a dark, stormy night; the wind blew a hurricane, and howled round the castle turrets, scattering the rain that between the gusts fell in torrents, in a kind of blinding mist, in all directions.

In one of the small wings or abutments of the court-yard, and near to the gate, was the laboratory of Doctor Crux.

This personage was an Italian, and even in those early days of chemical science, had, by continual research and experiments, arrived at a knowledge and skill that few could have overmatched.

He had come to England with Othniel, and it was to be feared his knowledge of one branch of chemistry—that of poisons—had been at various times unscrupulously made use of in carrying out the dark plans of his patron and master.

He was now engaged in distilling the juices from various herbs—a decoction of which was simmering in an iron vessel over a charcoal fire, whose fiery glare lighted up the chamber, and contrasted strongly with the bluish white flashes of the lightning, as it ever and anon played in wild revelry over the dark horizon.

The doctor, who has tried his skill upon the fair Algitha, was sorely perplexed to find that the draughts were not, in her case, possessed of the powers of the *elixir vitæ*.

Her consciousness had returned to her, but with it there also came a state of mental and bodily depression that was scarcely less objectionable than actual disease—in fact it *was* disease, but of a peculiar character—that sickness of the *mind* which is far more difficult to heal than that of the body.

"How the thunder rolls!" exclaimed the doctor, as he stirred up the herbs with a kind of fork, filling the apartment with a pungent, and by no means pleasant, odour.

The doctor, however, appeared to think otherwise, for he inhaled the effluvia with evident relish.

"Delicious!" he exclaimed, smacking his thin lips, as though he sought to taste it.

Peeping Tom, whom the doctor had seized upon, and pressed into his service as his drudge, thought otherwise, and was making unutterable faces in a corner, as he employed himself in cleaning certain dirty bottles.

"Delicious does he call it!" he said to himself, with a shudder; "I call it a awful stench. Oh! oh!" he exclaimed, as the doctor turned the compound over and over, and the vapour rose thicker than ever; "it's enough to make a fellow sick—ugh!"

Dr. Crux was compounding a love potion for Algitha, which was to have the double effect of restoring her to health and causing her to look favourably on her guardian, Lord Othniel.

Feeling that his medical skill was at stake, he was very anxious that his draught should be successful, and for that purpose he watched it with much assiduity.

Once more the elemental ordnance rang out across the plain, and "whoo-hooed" round the castle battlements, when, above the roar, there came upon his ear a cry for help.

At first he thought it must be fancy, but on listening, the cry was repeated.

"Help! help! for the love of the blessed saints, help!"

"My ears do not deceive me!" exclaimed the doctor; "it is indeed a human voice. Tommaso," he cried, addressing Tom, "Go out and see who it is that calls for help."

"Why does he call me Tommaso?" cried that worthy individual. "My name's Tom, without the *aso*. Does he mean to say I'm an ass?"

Tom thus soliloquised as he went out into the court-yard.

The night was indeed tempestuous. Though it was in the month of July, Nature save, from the leaves on the trees, gave no indication of the presence of summer. The sky was a dull, melancholy lead colour, and thick, dark clouds rolled rapidly athwart it, driven by the blast.

"What a night!" cried Tom, " to be out in."

He looked about in all directions, but saw nothing but drifting clouds, and heard nothing but the howling wind.

"There's no one there," he said, going to the door of the laboratory.

At this moment, as if giving the lie to the assertion, the cry was repeated.

"Help! help!"

"It comes from without the wall," remarked the physician. "Let us go and see."

Putting on a black skull cap to protect his head, and kindling a torch dipped in some inflammable material, he went forward to the gate, accompanied by Tom, who was not altogether sorry to exchange the fresh night air, boisterous as it was, for the *crux-ian* odours of the laboratory.

Drawing a key from his pouch, the physician opened a small door in the wall, and went out.

Holding the torch aloft, he looked hither and thither, and at length descried a huddled-up heap, that had the appearance of a human form.

"What is it?" said Tom, who perceived it at the same moment—" a wolf?"

Dr. Crux was a practical man, and simply replied—

"Go and see."

"But suppose," said Tom, apprehensively, "it *should* be a wolf, and he was to bite my head off, how then?"

"Why then, you'd be exactly a head shorter than you are at this moment," answered the physician.

Tom, not seeing anything satisfactory in such a prospect, did not offer to stir.

"You're afraid," said Dr. Crux. "I will go myself."

As he spoke, he advanced to where the supposed body was lying; Tom following at his heels, comforted with the idea that if it was a wolf, the physician would be the first to receive the benefit of his teeth.

It turned out as the doctor had supposed; it was a human being.

Giving the light to Tom, he stooped down and raised the head.

It was the body of a young man, from his appearance, scarcely twenty years of age.

He was pale as marble, and the dark masses of hair that fell over his shoulders, and the jetty fringes of his long eyelashes, added, by their contrast, an additional paleness to his features.

He was drenched, of course, to the skin, with rain, and presented a most forlorn appearance at that moment, although his dress and the beauty and whiteness of his hands dispelled any idea that he belonged to the mendicant class.

"This is no beggar," said the physician, as he bent down and applied a small bottle containing a powerful cordial to the young man's lips.

The effect was instantaneous.

A faint sigh burst from the youth, and his breast heaved with a deep inspiration.

"He lives, and will do well," soliloquized the chemist.

"Pr'aps he wants somethink to heat," suggested Tom.

"Perhaps," remarked the physician, "you will keep your suggestions till they are required, and in the meantime assist me to carry this young stranger into my apartment."

Tom, although snubbed by the Italian, professed his perfect willingness to make himself useful in any possible way, and by their joint efforts, the storm-beaten traveller was quickly removed to a place, if not of comfort, at least of warmth and shelter.

The physician, having removed his wet garments, placed him upon a couch that served for his own bed, and having administered a glass of generous wine, the combined action of this restorative and the genial warmth of the room speedily restored him to consciousness.

"Where am I?" he asked.

"You are in safety; that is sufficient for the present," replied the doctor, who began to take considerable interest in his patient.

This was not surprising, for never before had he seen a face so perfectly beautiful.

In addition to great regularity of feature, there was that mingled expression of boldness, vivacity, and sweetness in the large dark eyes, that betokened courage, chivalry, and great amiability of character.

As the meal proceeded, all reserve gradually disappeared, and the young stranger informed his preserver and host that though by birth English, he had lived some years in France, where he had studied the physician's art—that circumstances had induced him to return to his native country—that having landed on the coast he had procured a horse, which had been struck dead at some miles' distance from the castle, and that, having essayed the journey on foot on such a terrible night, he had become exhausted as he reached the castle walls.

Here was a pupil, a partner, such as he required—a kindred spirit that could enter into his scientific researches, and take an interest in his studies and pursuits, which the ignorant minds of those by whom he was surrounded could not.

It took but a short time to persuade the young stranger to domicile himself at the castle, and before they retired to rest that night, it was arranged that Almar—the name by which he called himself—should remain with Dr. Crux in the capacity of his assistant.

CHAPTER XX.

DOCTOR CRUX ADMINISTERS THE LOVE POTION, WHICH FAILS—ALMAR MAKES A SECOND EXPERIMENT AND SUCCEEDS — A JOYFUL MEETING—AN UGLY SPY—THE RIVALS—THE PRISONER.

SOME weeks passed, and still Algitha kept her chamber.

She complained of no pain, but appeared to sink down, into a state of quiet melancholy.

Lord Othniel kept aloof.

The love potion, so Doctor Crux informed him, was shortly to be administered, and would work a wonderful change.

But the doctor was mistaken.

The love potion was administered, but without the least effect.

Lord Othniel, on the strength of the physician's assurance, paid Algitha a visit, expecting to be received with rapture.

Great was his chagrin, therefore, at the reception he met with.

There was neither anger, fear, scorn, nor hate, simply a profound indifference, and he retired in disgust, to load Dr. Crux with execrations for so deceiving him.

The Italian, smarting under his own non-success, and the reproaches of his patron, was on bad terms with himself and all around him.

It was in vain his assistant pupil, Almar, endeavoured to draw him into some scientific argument—Dr. Crux was unapproachable.

His warm Italian blood was in a ferment. He felt he had made a failure, that he could not by any skill of his possibly rectify, and it filled him with the gall and wormwood of wounded pride.

Almar, who had witnessed the doctor's preparation of the love potion, and heard him speak in the most confident terms of its efficacy, was not slow to divine that it had been a total failure.

The impatient irritability of his master, his absent manner, and the angry tones of his voice, confirmed his opinion.

The doctor's chagrin at his failure was somewhat appeased on hearing from his assistant a flattering account of the ingredients which he had used.

"I should like myself to present a second draught," said Almar, "in every respect like the first, to your fair patient; then, if it failed to work an immediate cure, I should own myself egregiously mistaken, but not till then."

"You shall have the opportunity, my dear young friend. I can promise that," said the doctor.

"The only stipulations I make, in order to ensure success, is, that no one be in the room at the time I present it but the patient and myself."

"That also can be complied with," answered the Italian.

"Then prepare the draught and hope the best."

The next day the Lady Algitha was informed that Doctor Almar, a young physician of high repute, would visit her, bringing with him a draught that would infallibly restore her to her wonted health and spirits.

Algitha made no opposition, and the time appointed for the interview drew near.

Almar at this crisis, entered the room.

Sinking on one knee by the side of the couch, he gently clasped the fair hand, and, in a gentle tone, murmured her name—

"Algitha!"

With a cry of joy, the maiden turned and gazed upon him, as though she could scarcely believe she was not in a dream.

"Rupert! my own Rupert! my beloved!" she cried, in delirious joy, as she threw her white arms round his neck.

"And do I hold you to my heart once more, my Algitha?" murmured the young man.

"You are here, Rupert, and I am now quite well."

"But you are pale, dearest; you have been ill, very ill, have you not?" inquired Rupert, with tender solicitude.

"I have been in danger, terrible danger; but you are here, and I am safe."

"Danger, love! From whom?"

"From him to whom my parents entrusted me—my guardian, the custodian of this castle."

Had Algitha or Rupert been less absorbed in each other, they might have seen the malicious yellow face of Ghoul at the window.

The dwarf gave a spiteful grin, and almost immediately disappeared.

"Has this guardian dared to insult you love?" inquired Rupert, indignantly.

"He has deeply; but now you are here I fear him no longer."

"The traitor! He shall answer to me for the sufferings he has caused you!" cried Rupert.

"Think not of it, dearest," she exclaimed; "'tis over now, and for myself, I can forget all that is past in contemplating my present joy—your loved presence."

"But Rupert was not so easily appeased. He

chafed under the insults offered to the fair girl he worshipped.

"Tell me all, dearest ; hide nothing from me," he entreated.

Thus adjured, she related all that had passed, to Rupert's unbounded indignation.

She endeavoured to calm him, and as a means to an end led him on to recount the reason of his leaving France.

"Was not your departure a sufficient plea to induce me to follow ?"

"And your arrival here—how strange, how providential ! Depend upon it, heaven sent you hither to be my protector."

"As I will be, so long as life shall last," exclaimed Rupert, pressing her to his bosom.

At this moment the door suddenly opened, and Othniel, followed by the dwarf and four armed men, entered.

"What means this, insolent villain ?" he shouted to Rupert.

"It means," returned the young man, fiercely, "that you are a false knight: that you have dishonoured a sacred trust ; and that I am here to supply your place."

"Ho! ho!" sneered Othniel," you here ?—*you !* —a doctor's assistant—a spreader of plasters and pounder of drugs ! A very choice association ! Away with him !"

Rupert was overpowered and borne to the ground by the four heavily-mailed guards.

"Away with the insolent charlatan," he cried, contemptuously. "Convey him to the deepest dungeon."

They were about to obey, when Algitha rushed forward.

"Lord Othniel," she cried, "I understand you now ; your deeds speak for you. You are a villain ; but I fear you not. I am the daughter of a brave sire and a noble mother, and I charge you to release that gentleman "—pointing to Rupert.

"Ha! ha! fair maiden ; I am master here. Away with him !"

He waved his hand as he spoke, and Rupert was dragged away to a dungeon.

Othniel was once more alone with his ward.

"You will repent these outrages, my lord !" she cried. "The same Providence that has preserved me once can help me still—and now leave me."

"I obey you for the present," Othniel replied. "I will leave you ; but you will see me again, when, perhaps, your tone will change."

With a look of mingled anger and derision, he left the apartment.

———

CHAPTER XXI.

LORD OTHNIEL RESOLVES TO RID HIMSELF OF HIS RIVAL—THE POISONED FOOD—WICKED DESIGNS FRUSTRATED.

DR. CRUX, who had heard of the miraculous cure that had been effected in the Lady Algitha, was utterly confounded at the treatment his *protegée* had received.

He remonstrated in vain with the jealous and vindictive Othniel, who, having his rival in his power, resolved to seize the golden opportunity, and rid himself of him at once and for ever.

He resolved in his mind the best way to dispatch him.

He at last determined on poison, as being more secret and no less certain in its operation.

"I can procure the deadly mineral from the Italian," he soliloquized, "without informing him for whom I need it. The body can be removed at night, and it can be reported he has escaped."

Othniel appeared quite relieved after he had arranged this vile plot, and at once sought Dr. Crux.

The doctor, having been made acquainted with the wishes of his villanous master, and expressing compunction at the deed—for the last victim of his accursed art had so impressed him by his dying agony, that he had made a vow never again to be made the tool of Othniel in sending a fellow creature to his account—at last yielded to the taunts of his employer, and furnished him with the deadly potion.

Othniel received it eagerly, with a fiendish exultation sparkling in his dark eye, and instantly departed.

His lordship filled a plate with some of the choicest portions, with which he thoroughly mingled the powder he had received from Dr. Crux.

He summoned Tom Winker to his presence.

Tom proceeded to the dining-room, and tapped at the door.

"Approach !" said his master.

Tom, who had a faint idea that he was going to be asked to dinner, smacked his lips at the savoury odour of viands, and, drawing a chair to the table, sat down very composedly.

"Who ordered you to sit down, knave?" cried his lordship. "Stand up, sirrah !"

"I allus perfers takin' my meals sittin'," remarked Tom, innocently.

Othniel seized him by the collar indignantly, and jerked him out of the chair with an impetus that almost deprived him of consciousness.

"Idiot !" exclaimed the incensed nobleman, "do you imagine I should ever invite scum as thou art to my table ? Learn to know yourself and your position."

Tom's position at that moment was peculiar. His toes were turned in, and his hands were turned out, and his fat face and goggle eyes presented an unutterable comic appearance.

"Listen to me," cried his master.

Tom opened both his eyes immediately.

"This stranger," commenced Othniel—" this Rupert has glaringly offended me, and for this offence I have incarcerated him in the vault beneath the castle."

"I know yer 'as," broke in Tom ; "and that ugly Ghoul's jailor, he likes that."

"Silence, and don't interrupt me," cried Othniel, "and as I consider it beneath me to stretch my displeasure to more than an equivalent punishment, therefore you will take this plate of food and this flagon of wine to Ghoul, who keeps guard at the dungeon door, and order him to take it to the prisoner within, but on no account to say to whose kindness he owes so dainty a repast. Let him consider to any one rather than to me."

"I'll say as Una sent it," said Tom.

"Yes, that will do ; and now begone at once upon your errand."

Tom took up the plate and the flagon and departed, whilst the guilty Othniel threw himself back in his chair, and emptied a goblet of wine.

Tom proceeded to the spot where Ghoul, in anything but a good humour, kept guard over the prisoner.

"Are you there?" cried Tom.

"Can't you see?" growled the dwarf.

"There's nothin' of yer to see," politely remarked Tom; "besides, if there was, it's so precious dark 'ere."

"What d'ye want, now you're come?"

"I've brought some dinner," said Tom.

The dwarf's harsh features relaxed into an hungry smile.

"Dinner!" he cried; "it's about time; I'm half-starved."

"It ain't for you," replied Tom, "and mind you don't go a eatin' it."

"Mind your own business," ejaculated the dwarf, grinding his teeth.

Tom, who had quite enough of the dark passages, returned to Una, while Ghoul stood soliloquizing with the plate in one hand and the wine in the other.

"Now, if I were a prisoner, Lord Othniel wouldn't send me any choice food or wine, not he! He'd rather see me starve. Didn't he rob me of the purse to-day? he did—he did. If he took my purse I have a right to this dinner, and I'll have it too;" and so, without further ado, he squatted down on the ground and demolished it with great relish, assisting its downward passage by draughts of wine.

In a very short time he had effected a clearance, and folding his arms composed himself for a nap.

In the meantime Othniel, gloating over the success of his villanous plan, sat quaffing his wine in his own chamber, when, suddenly, as the fumes of the liquid mounted to his brain, a fiendish thought struck him, that it would be a choice spectacle to watch the dying agonies of his infuriated rival.

He accordingly started from his seat, and kindling a taper, reeled from the apartment, making his way to the dungeon below.

On arriving at the door, the first object that met his gaze was the dwarf in a happy state of unconsciousness—being fast asleep—and the empty plate and flagon standing by his side.

"How now, thou puny whelp!" he shouted; "is it thus you keep your guard? Awake!"

And as he spoke, he applied his foot to the dwarf's ribs, who howled vociferously.

Seeing who it was, he sprang to his feet.

"Has the prisoner had the food I sent him?" he inquired.

"Yes, my lord," answered Ghoul, unhesitatingly.

"And he enjoyed it?"

"Very much, your lordship; he could have eaten some more if he had had it,' replied the dwarf, with a grin at his own facetiousness.

"He will find that sufficient," muttered Othniel to himself.

Taking a key from his pouch he opened the massive door and entered.

He held aloft the taper, and peered into the surrounding darkness.

"He must be dead," he murmured under his breath. "This poison does its work quickly."

He gazed down upon the prostrate youth, but the regular rise and fall of his ample chest proved him not only not dead, but full of the breath of life.

The guilty miscreant marvelled.

The young man stirred, and, aroused by the light, started from his sleep.

"Who's there?" he cried.

"One who knows how to crush a rival when he finds him crawling in his path," was the insulting answer.

"You know that I am powerless," he cried, "or you would not dare to insult me."

"Insult!" replied Othniel, ironically. "Methinks you ought to give me credit for the courtesy I have shown you. It is not *every* prisoner I supply with wine and meat from my own table."

"Wine and meat," echoed Rupert. "Say rather bread and water."

"I say meat and wine," repeated Othniel, positively. "I served you with my own hands, and sent it. Did you not receive it?"

"If you are not jesting," answered Rupert, "I can assure you the favours you intended for me have not arrived as yet;" adding, in an under tone, "perhaps it is as well for me they have not."

"But," said Othniel, suddenly, "I saw the plate and flagon empty outside the dungeon door. Some one must have "——

His speech was interrupted by a succession of wild yells, and hastily going to the door, he found the dwarf Ghoul writhing in all the agony in which he hoped to have discovered Rupert.

"What is the matter, abortion?" he shouted.

"I know not!" shrieked the dwarf. "I'm in torture—agony! Oh! oh!" and he rolled over and over on the ground, groaning lamentably.

"Have you eaten from that plate, or drank from that cup!" inquired Othniel, in a stern voice.

"I have! I have!" yelled the dwarf.

"I can tell you, then, the cause of the pains that rack you—*you are poisoned!*"

A prolonged yell followed up this announcement, and Othniel locked the prison door, and returned to his own chamber to meditate some fresh villany.

CHAPTER XXII.

A CURE FOR POISON—THE ASSASSIN—AN UNEXPECTED VISITOR—THE RESCUE.

As the guilty man sank into a seat, and plunged once more into the Lethean wine-cup, his designs, far from causing him remorse, only embittered him, inasmuch as they had fallen short of the end he intended.

At length he started up, and strode across the apartment.

"Away, remorse!" he cried. "This night shall witness my rival's destruction, and the fair Algitha clasped in these arms."

His hand rested on the cabinet where he had placed the arrow, on which was the stern inscription—"BEWARE THE GREY MONK!"

"Psha!" he cried. "Grey Monk! Fiend! Demon! or whatsoe'er thou art, I defy thee!"

A mocking, hollow laugh, that issued, seemed to answer him.

"Fool!" it cried. "Beware!"

In spite of himself, these words, uttered in a deep, low, solemn tone, filled him with a mysterious terror he could not repress.

It seemed like a warning from the lips of fate.

By a strong mental effort, he shook off his terrors, and drank still deeper than before.

The wretched Ghoul, in the meantime, lay writhing and groaning at the prison door.

He firmly believed his doom was sealed.

"Had I not eaten of that accursed dish!" he groaned, "I should now be well and strong. Curse him! May his hand wither that mingled death with that which heaven gave for life!"

He resolved ere his breath fled to ixpose the deed of Othniel.

"The murderer shall be unmasked," he said. "The poisoner!"

With trembling hands he dragged himself along the gloomy passages, pausing every now and then, as the terrible pains racked him.

At length he reached the kitchen where Tom, in his anxiety to assist Una, had heaped fuel upon the fire until the water in the copper bubbled and hissed furiously.

"Ain't this prime?" he said to Una. "I like to see the water boil."

At this moment a dismal groaning was heard outside the door of the kitchen, and Ghoul, pale and ghastly, rolled into the apartment.

"What's the matter?" said Tom.

"I'm poisoned!" groaned the dwarf.

"Who poisoned yer?" Tom inquired.

"That infernal villain, Othniel! Oh! oh!" he groaned. "He poisoned the meat, and I—I, fool that I was, I ate it!"

"What!" cried Tom. "D'ye mean to say as that meat was pisoned?"

"I do. Oh, that I had not tasted it!"

"But I tasted it too!" roared Tom, "and I shall die as well. Oh! oh! oh!" And he threw himself on the floor and kicked.

"You must both take an emetic," cried Una.

"What's that?" groaned Tom and the dwarf simultaneously.

"Hot soap-suds," returned Una. "There's plenty in the copper."

There was an immediate rush to this receptacle. Ghoul, in spite of his pangs, sprang on to the top of the copper.

"You're not a-goin' to drink it all!" yelled Tom.

They felt their safety was comprised in copious draughts of soap-suds.

The struggle for the first draught was tremendous.

Suddenly, however, a loud explosion was heard.

The copper boiler—the steam having no outlet for escape—had burst, and the poisoned victims, Tom and the dwarf, were blown up in the air.

On alighting they looked up. They saw the pale features of Doctor Crux.

"You will not die," said the doctor, to the dwarf and Tom, after Una had explained matters, "but let this be a lesson to you not to taste what does not belong to you."

It was midnight. All was silent in the castle.

All slept but the guilty Othniel, whose fierce passions banished sleep from his couch.

Rupert slept calmly on his straw pallet in his dungeon.

Suddenly a small door in the wall opened silently.

A man appeared, carrying a light and a dagger.

He approached the unconscious sleeper, little dreaming he was followed by a form clad in a grey gown and hood, which concealed his features.

The assassin was Karl, of Brabant.

He raised the glittering steel, and as it was about to descend, a powerful grasp seized his wrist, and a firm voice cried—

"Your own doom is your reward, assassin!"

The guilty wretch gave a terrific cry, as his eyes fell upon the grinning face of a SKELETON.

The blow descended, and the murderer fell to the ground, a corpse.

Rupert started from his slumber, and as the mask fell from the face of the friar, exclaimed—

"Father!"

"My boy!" warmly returned the friar.

A cry from Algitha then reached their ears.

"Follow me," exclaimed the monk, unlocking the fetters from his waist.

They had now reached a small door.

"Mercy! mercy!" cried a voice within.

It was Algitha's voice.

"You plead in vain," exclaimed Othniel.

At this moment a fierce blast of a trumpet was heard, and a rush of many footsteps.

Othniel released his prey and staggered back. A door, concealed by drapery, burst asunder, and he found himself facing the *Grey Monk*.

"Brother!" he gasped—"Reginald!"

"Ay!" returned the friar, "that brother falsely accused and dispossessed of his estates by your treachery, but whose innocence is now proven, and who is now restored by order of the noble Richard."

Appalled, the guilty Othniel stood glaring at his injured brother.

"Not by my hand will your punishment fall," continued Reginald Raven. "Guilty as you are, you are my brother."

A body of soldiers entered the chamber, and the guilty brother was removed.

The beautiful Algitha was restored to her mother, the Lady Godiva, whose death had been simply a *ruse* to escape the designs of Othniel.

The blow of the villain Wolfhart was frustrated by Eric, and the gallant Leofric returned from Palestine to meet his beloved wife and child once more, the latter becoming the wife of Rupert.

Our friend Tom and the dwarf became in course of time old cronies—the former leading the pretty Una to the altar, but never till his dying day did he regret the hour when he entered the service of Earl Leofric and the Lady Godiva.

THE END.

*   *   *   *   *   *